THE MOSS HOUSE

THE MOSS HOUSE

A novel by
Clara Barley

Bluemoose

Copyright © Clara Barley 2019

First published in 2019 by
Bluemoose Books Ltd
25 Sackville Street
Hebden Bridge
West Yorkshire
HX7 7DJ

www.bluemoosebooks.com

British Library Cataloguing-in-Publication data
A catalogue record for this book is available from the British Library

Hardback ISBN 978-1-910422-50-2

Paperback 978-1-910422-49-6

Printed and bound in the UK by Short Run Press

As our warm bodies and lips press together,
I finally feel free, content and, dare I say it, in love again.
I pull back to look down into my lover's eyes and,
hoping to see the same reflected back at me, I see instead
the opposite. I realise that Miss Walker has everything
a woman could ever desire to be happy except the
very power to enjoy it, and there is nothing I can ever
do to change that.

Chapter One

Summer, 1832: A chance reunion at Shibden Hall

Miss Lister

Marry a man? I would rather die.

It is the worst thing I could imagine, both physically and emotionally. It would be the end of every freedom I have worked so hard to achieve. Why would I even dream of handing over my property and liberty to some swine who will drink and gamble it away and make poor investments, whilst I – what, stay at home and sew? Push out mewling babies and let my mind slowly deteriorate through lack of stimulation? Never. Yet women I would call my equals in both mind and ambition have succumbed. Women I have bedded and aroused and pledged love to. Women who would never need a man's money or power, who could have lived here with me at Shibden Hall and never had want of anything, have succumbed. It must be for some innate desire of theirs that I seem to have been born without, to be – what? Owned? I cannot understand it. It is the cause of my ultimate frustration; I have lost more than one love to it. Is there a lure to becoming a Mrs and losing one's own name? A lure to being taken, possessed? I do not understand it.

She will be here at two o'clock: Miss Walker, my potential new lover. It will be hard work to woo her, I'm sure – I just hope she will be worth it. She already vexes me. But she fits nicely into my scheme of things. Fancy, I have travelled to other countries and had dozens of lovers and even had a marriage ceremony with my dear Mariana, only to find myself back here in Yorkshire at my family home of Shibden Hall, stumbling across a pretty girl living just next door to my family's estate. It seems foolish really, like a made-up story, to have been so close to her all these years and yet failed to meet her despite countless opportunities. I suppose I have been away travelling far too much to ever be here long, to ever really settle before now. She told me we met once before, a long time ago, but I barely remember the meeting and certainly did not notice her back then. She is years younger than me and I was no doubt madly in love with Mariana at the time.

I wonder if I had happened across her sooner, if our lives had entwined before now, would I have fallen for her then? What person would I now be? Would we be sitting here side by side, barely a word between us, like elderly couples who hardly bother about the other, or bicker with each other about trivial things, or get to the age where neither can hear the other and so cease speaking altogether? How tiresome to think of that. If I secure Miss Walker as my partner then perhaps that is what will be in store. Will she rile me? Will the sound of her breathing make me tense, not with passion but with annoyance? She will make trite embroidered items and we will have boring guests for tea and make small talk and we shall be known as the Ladies of Shibden Hall. Or the Ladies of Halifax.

We met again only last week when her aunt brought her over for a visit, her Aunt Walker whom we've not seen or heard from for years. She said she was bringing her niece over to cheer her up, though they did not tell us what she needed cheering up from, and no doubt to question what I have been up to these years in France. After tea and pleasantries, noticing how she would catch my eye then look away, I took her for a short stroll around the grounds and before I could stop myself, making sure no one would see us, I drew her close to me and kissed her. She did not resist.

Now she comes again to visit. She was evidently not deterred. Shame her aunt is coming too. I am anxious for 2 o'clock to arrive.

I am torn between settling here at my home of Shibden once and for all and embracing all I can do with the estate and local life, or setting off around the world, never to return. I remember Paris and my younger self's ambitions. I studied anatomy...

I could disguise myself as a man and go somewhere where no one knows me. I could be a scholar, a doctor even. Use the income from Shibden to rent a place of my own, alone. Create a new identity. A new life as a man. I could be Doctor Lister – a John, Samuel or Jeremy.

Could I truly live in disguise, with the constant fear of discovery? Would any woman want me if I dressed as a man? They'd have to know my secret at some point. Am I more attractive to them as a woman? I believe I have avoided attracting attention to my relationships because as two women we are seen as merely close friends. But as a man, I would have to court just one woman and marry her before we could so much as touch each other's skin under our clothes. With women, well, I can undress them and take them and it's as if no harm is done. Their reputation is unsullied. The only damage is that I get hurt. Each time I imagine that this one will be the one, that this woman will love me as much as I love her, that this woman will not succumb to marriage, that this woman will be content with me and we will live our lives together – but each one, in turn, torments herself with her feelings for me and turns back to what is expected of her. Except poor Isabella, who loved me and would be here now beside me – but she is the only one I couldn't love. Fate is cruel sometimes. I believe she feels for me as I feel for Mariana: a love that rises in your chest when you see them, hear their voice, receive a letter. A love that occupies your mind. A face that fills your vision when you close your eyes and is there every time you touch yourself, and every time you take pleasure, no matter whom you are with. Oh, Mariana. That Heaven should practice stratagems against so soft a subject as myself.

But Mariana is out of my reach now, and who is left but Miss Walker? She who will be here at two o'clock with her handsome face and shy demeanour and polite conversation. On our short stroll last week, it did not take long for her to confess to me that she does not wish to marry a man, clearly wanting to align herself to my own spinsterhood. Or something else? I tried my luck with a kiss. I believe she will make a good companion, if nothing else. I am forty-one years old and I fear she is my last chance. It is not that I am heartless, but the practicalities of my situation seem to have come to the forefront of my thoughts these days. I feel I have wasted some twenty years or more pursuing this woman or that, and forever being spurned; and though I have enjoyed my adventures, the clock ticks on and my diary pages fill up and I am still a spinster whose fear is that I will be alone and unloved, and never achieve happiness.

From now on I will try to thrust myself into work on the Hall and estate and embed myself in Halifax life and society, though some days I just want to run out of the door, through the courtyard, down the lane and head... where? I know not. Some days I dream of being anywhere but here. But this new acquaintance at least gives me something to think upon. Could Miss Walker be a reason to stay?

Miss Walker

My heart races already and I still have an hour before I leave for Shibden. She has a power over me. I fear her and long for her in equal measure. I fear for how I will act, what I will say. I fear I will blush and my aunt will see it written across my face that I have let this woman kiss me. That I have let her kiss me passionately. That I did not resist but kissed her back, for in her presence I feel more alive than I have ever felt. Her confidence radiates and envelops me and gives me a strength I can only remember from when I was very young. Before... before life took hold of me.

I try to compose myself and act as if it is just another social call. Just a new friend with whom I shall have tea and talk, and leave as if it is nothing – but I keep thinking of that kiss. Of the way she looked at me. And smiled. And drew closer to me. And I was excited. And although I knew what was going to happen, it still caught me unawares. And I thought for a moment that I would recoil, but my body did the opposite; it leaned in and a heat rose in me and all the world around me disappeared and for those moments I was lost, swimming in the middle of a wide ocean. I was lost but found. Found but lost.

I feel my pulse racing at the thought of her. How I long to kiss her again, but it only occurred because we happened to be alone. My aunt insists on accompanying me again today; I believe she just wants to pry at Shibden Hall and seek a better acquaintance with the Lister family. I wonder if I will even be able to look Miss Lister in the eye without blushing, without stammering my words. Without fainting.

Do I fear her? Or desire her? Or fear the fact that I long for her? It is strictly forbidden for men to kiss each other; I can only assume the same is for women. It will be very frowned upon.

I am already the ridicule of the Walker family, the prosperous manufacturers and merchants, related to every elite family in Halifax.

Despite my inheritance, I have not found an appropriate suitor and remain single at twenty-nine. I have turned men down, much to my family's dismay. But why should I marry? I ask over and over. Why should I hand over my wealth and independence to someone else? Why cannot I just... be alone? I suppose I would be, if it weren't for Miss Lister. After our chance reunion, whereby my aunt suggested we reacquaint ourselves with our neighbour who has returned from overseas travels – and suddenly my small world has been turned upside down, for a thought has entered my head that I would never have dared to imagine. My options were to marry a man, or to spend my life alone. But now, because of a kiss, I dare to wonder that perhaps there is a third option. An option that may provide a happiness I have never before imagined. I could remain independent but have the company I crave, and not just company, but excitement, and, dare I say it, pleasure.

But who am I to deserve happiness?

My maid enters and checks my hair and I cannot look her in the eye. I fear that I have a look of guilt upon my face at just the thought of Miss Lister. Is the kiss we shared to be a burden on me for the rest of my days? Am I branded a deviant already? Will God judge me and condemn me? Oh, how my mind races. I must focus on now, right now. I must get up and leave this room. Go downstairs and greet my aunt and act casually about the visit and put on my cloak and then mount the carriage and make small talk with my aunt about the weather and the horses and the condition of the roads and Miss Lister and her younger sister Miss Marian Lister and her Aunt Anne and father, and how we mustn't stay too long in case the weather turns and hope, just hope, that nothing in my demeanour or what I say will reveal me. Reveal that I am as nervous as a schoolgirl, as nervous as when I first danced in public, as nervous as when a boy first touched my hand, as when a boy first kissed me. With Miss Lister, though, it is not just nerves but a thrill.

I realise. Why didn't I think of it sooner? This is what it feels like to fall in love. But not just any love. A secret love. A forbidden love.

I begin to worry that she does not feel the same, that I am just a conquest and will be cast aside. Perhaps she will go off travelling again and will leave me here, alone, never knowing, ever waiting for her to return.

These are the thoughts that possess me all the way to Shibden Hall, right up until the moment I see her standing there in the doorway, her hand raised in greeting. Suddenly all the thoughts stop, and it is just her looking at me, and me looking back at her, and I no longer care about anything, past or future, just being here right now. The thought that crashes to the front of my mind then is simply: please kiss me again.

Miss Lister

I read on her face that she is smitten. She does not need to utter the words. I wonder if others can read it too? Not likely her aunt, who never looks anyone in the eye as she's so busy talking about herself and asking Father about the estate and goings-on in Halifax. My aunt may recognise the glances between us, but if she does, she turns a blind eye. My sister Marian, however, sits like my own private judge, constantly watching me. Although she makes no sound, I can hear her

7

tutting. I wonder if she suspects, though I do not much care if she does.

I watch Miss Walker; she is very attractive, more than I had first thought, but she seems to be ashamed of her attractiveness, and in feeling so, she decreases it. She holds herself well enough, but she is one of those whose size you cannot determine. She could be my height, but she seems small. As if apologising for taking up as much space as God created her to take up.

As I sit here in my usual black clothing, which I chose to wear some twenty years ago and have rarely wavered from since, I see that we are opposites in some ways and alike in others. Alike in how we may feel about each other, assuming the kiss is anything to go by and that the signals I am now reading are correct. Alike in that we are independent and have our own means of wealth, and alike in that neither of us has need nor, I believe, the desire to marry a man – but we are opposite in every other way. Today, with her dress so pale, we are like ebony and ivory. Precious Miss Walker, 'of fragile body and mind' as she was described to me by our mutual friend Mrs Priestley. Fragile mind, as if it should break open any moment and what would be released? Brains or butterflies? I have seen inside a brain and am in awe of its construction; how such an ugly mass can create us as individuals and, in turn, allow us to create and see beauty around us. Beauty that Miss Walker possesses.

I wonder what she sees when she looks at me? Does she look down on Gentleman Jack, as I am called by those who disrespect me? Perhaps I am actually flattered by the name, that I should become enough of a man in their eyes to be in need of a name to explain it. Has she even heard this name, I wonder? I bet her nosy aunt would be ashamed to be associated with Gentleman Jack. But if she were, she would not have visited again surely? They cannot know of it. It is a shame we both share the same Christian name of Anne. It will be strange if we become close that we will call each other by our own names, the only difference being that my Anne has an 'e'. But for now, as society dictates, she will remain Miss Walker to me, and I Miss Lister to her.

I think I shall take the name Gentleman Jack as mine. Privately, as we sit listening to our aunts talk nonsense, we catch each other's eyes again and I imagine her naked on top of me as I lie in my bed, her hair loose and free from its curls. She looks at me and whispers, my Gentleman Jack, and then leans down to press her lips hard against mine.

Marian asks me something about the estate and I have to ask her to repeat the question. When I look again at Miss Walker she is blushing, as if she had had the very same daydream. I decide I shall ask her, in time, to call me Gentleman Jack.

In the meantime I must sit through this tedium of visiting, but I make sure I catch hold of her hand as she leaves and let my lips brush against her cheek as I feel her tense and she holds my gaze. I think I shall be able to have my way with her. I need to plot a way to be alone with her again, and this time when I kiss her, I will ask her what she feels. Many girls like to be kissed but that is all. The moment you suggest more, with a wandering hand to their breast or thigh, they become embarrassed, and I must laugh and smile as if it were just a joke and hide my hurt that they only want so much of me. They want a kiss from me, but not a kiss down there. That's territory you must work towards slowly. Test the waters. Have those conversations about men and women and bodies and carnal pleasure and God, et cetera, until you're sure that they are thinking what you're thinking. Then... well. Then you can start to have some fun.

Miss Walker

Back at home, my mind races. How can I orchestrate another meeting without our families all around? I must be calm. I may just be one of her conquests. She will cast me aside if I kiss her again too quickly. Perhaps she collects kisses?

I have never met a woman like her and doubt I ever will again. I have had female friends before, of course, but none like her that make me feel... alive. Is it a sin to feel this way? About another woman, indeed, when surely I should be longing for a man's company and attention?

It felt as though we were sitting miles apart. Just when I had convinced myself that I had imagined our previous encounter and that there was no chance of it occurring again, as we left she touched my hand, pulled me close and her lips brushed against my cheek. I know I blushed. I fairly staggered into the carriage. I wonder if my aunt noticed, or Miss Lister's aunt or sister, or any of the servants who watch us closely and no doubt judge us? But what harm is it, for two women to have some affection between them? Two single women at that. We are not having an affair or causing a scandal, so why does the thought of her cause a fear in me? That perhaps there is more than just a kiss on her mind? Or am I more afraid that she *only* wants a kiss from me and then it will be done? I fear I will receive no letter or invitation and she will head off again on her travels and never give me a second thought.

She has mainly lived in France for several years now. I should like to see it. I've never had much opportunity to travel. My family has surrounded me and kept me occupied with trivial visits and letter writing and are always trying to turn my opinion this way or that, suggesting various men with whom I could become acquainted.

Some days I wish I'd never inherited the Walker estate. The grief of losing both my parents at just nineteen was never worth this turmoil. I long for them to be back with me. I wish my father had advised my sister Elizabeth and me on what we should do, but he passed quickly and my mother shortly afterwards. Then we lost our dear brother too. To this day I still do not know the full length and breadth of the estate I inherited, although I know it must be large, given the way my family circles around me, all wanting a piece, all telling me that if I do not marry the estate will be broken up and lost − as if I should care what happens after I die!

My sister married but I detest her husband. He looks down upon me, as if I am always in the way. He knows that if I were to die then he would get the entire estate. Poor Elizabeth thought she had married well, but he soon showed his true colours. They barely spend any time together now and he gives her a meagre allowance from her own money, which she handed over to him when she took her vows. Why would I ever seek to do the same? I could not bear to hand over the freedom I now have to a man and be forever dependent on his charity and good favour. Like Elizabeth, I would be expected to produce children, the very thought of which horrifies me. I worry that my body would never cope with such pressures. Some days it hurts me just to stand as my back is so fragile, I feel so weak. I saw my cousin grow so big she could barely walk! I've heard the screams of childbirth and no descriptions of it as a miracle could encourage me to endure such pain. I've seen the exhausted faces of new mothers, seen them with screaming creatures in their arms who then grow to run around with no concern for their poor mother, who loses her figure, her health and her very self by enduring to produce them.

Yet just a short while past I agreed to do just that. I shall not think of him too much or I shall begin to weep. I am grateful to my aunt for making me leave the house with her to help take my mind off things. I shall think of Miss Lister instead and focus on contriving a way to meet her again without our families present. I will suggest a walk together.

A small part of me thinks perhaps I am playing with fire, but I have been burned before and survived.

Chapter Two

Summer, 1832: An interfering aunt and secret kisses

Miss Lister

That damnable woman! How dare she interfere and suggest that I am inappropriate company for her niece? Miss Walker confides in me after she comes over alone and spends a pleasant morning with me and we take a walk in the woods that her aunt seems to have changed her mind about our new friendship. She has tired of us Listers already after just two visits and warns Miss Walker away. What a changeable character! Does she not know who I am? I am perfectly adequate company for her meek mannered and uneducated niece who blushes at the very sight of me. Lead her astray indeed! She cannot possibly know that we kissed. We were on a walk far from any prying eyes. Someone must have been watching us and reported back to that chitter-chatterer of a woman, who has nothing to do but interfere in her niece's life in the hopes of some pittance of her inheritance, living off her while pretending to be her companion and protector. The sooner I can be rid of her meddling influence the better. Inappropriate company indeed! I wager this is the first time poor little Miss Walker has ever had a decent conversation in her life that did not revolve around the weather and dresses and children and pitiful society. These nouveaux riches seem to forget how lucky they are when they could easily have been born to poverty, where little Miss Walker would have been working in the mills from five years old.

I must find out if someone told on us and shoot them! Unless... unless it was Miss Walker herself. Could she be so foolish as to confide in her silly aunt? If that is the case, then we are doomed never to exchange more than pleasantries at church. Lead her astray, she said! I believe leading astray is exactly what Miss Walker needs. She certainly does not resist my kisses on our second walk.

I do not know how I have let this rile me so much. Normally such gossip and hearsay are water off a duck's back to me. I've been the subject of gossip before – how I dress, how I manage my affairs, even how I walk. Protective mothers and aunts may warn their charges to not get too close to Miss Lister. Perhaps I really care this time? Care that Miss Walker might be snatched away from me before I get any further than a bit of kissing. I know well she liked it. She couldn't stop herself. We could have kissed for hours until our faces were sore and we were too exhausted to continue. Of course, I left it at just a kiss again, kept my hands only on her arms and lower back and her gentle little neck. All very decent of me while growing hot down there and having to contain myself so that I may leave her wanting more. I asked her how she felt, and she seemed to think I was unlike any woman she had known. How unsurprised I was at that. She asked if what we were doing was wrong, so I reassured her greatly that we were just enjoying something pleasurable and two unattached ladies were more than permitted to enjoy a small amount of pleasure every now and then.

I know for sure now she is keen on me. It was she who arranged our second walk, knowing full well we would be alone. Despite her aunt's warning, she showed no resistance at all when I held her hand and drew her close to me, but if she is going to question what is wrong at just a kiss, I wonder if this adventure may take a long time to progress to anything close to proper pleasure. Will she be worth it? I'm not sure. She certainly kisses well, passionately and deeply, and is not afraid to use her tongue and nip at my lips with her teeth. She presses hard into my neck and back with her delicate hands as if wanting us to merge into one. I believe I will eventually have my way with her. I believe she wants it too.

But now her scheming aunt warns her away from me. Miss Walker has ignored her, but the seeds of doubt may have been sown. I should invite them both over for a visit and be on my best and most charming behaviour with them, reassure them that I intend only friendship. Or I could ignore them both for a few weeks. Let them stew. If Miss Walker is intent on seeing me again and having me kiss her, then I shall leave it to her to do the chasing. Yes, I shall leave it to her to decide if she wishes to see me again. Although I am keen on her, she is not the only woman in Yorkshire left for me, though it would be most convenient if I could secure her company as she is very pleasing to look at. However, I cannot put all my wager on her, especially if she may be easily distracted from her course by a few words from a nosy aunt.

I am decided then. I shall carry on my business as usual and focus on the Hall and the running of the estate. While Miss Walker sits daintily by as others conduct her business, I have Shibden to manage which is a full-time occupation. There is work on the grounds to complete, inspections of our lands; I must oversee the coal mines, stone and timber reserves, ensure our finances are in order with incomes from our canal and road shares and visit our tenants in need of support.

I shall send the Walkers no invitation but contrive to make sure they hear of me visiting others in the area and being seen about town. I will visit our mutual friend Mrs Priestley again and she will then no doubt tell of my visit when she next sees the Walkers as she rarely keeps anything to herself. That will make her come running to me.

Miss Walker

I know I shouldn't, but I lock myself in my bedroom and without even undressing, let my hand find its way up under my skirts and through my drawers and find my hot, damp hair. I gently part my lips and rub the moisture around them, close them with my fingers and slowly start to circle and circle, gently and steadily at first and then, as I gather speed, my other hand clutches at one of my breasts and squeezes it hard as my breath quickens and my heart pulses in my ears. I close my eyes to the world around me and focus in on that one small place and the rhythm of my hand as I feel my body tensing and a pleasure slowly growing behind my fingers, and it grows and grows as I rub harder and faster, my arm aching and my other hand now reaching down too, pushing my skirts up so it can grab hold of my thigh and grip hard, my nails biting into my skin as my hand circles and circles and then my breath catches and my whole body shudders with pleasure emanating out from that small spot, throughout my entire self, spreading out through my arms and legs and head like lighting has struck me, and I sink back into the waves of pleasure. I let go with both my hands and lie there, legs apart, eyes still closed.

After just a moment's respite, I want more. My fingers find the spot again, and start to gently caress once more, and within a few moments the heat rises again, and another shock of pleasure emanates up through my body, almost as good as the first. I squeeze my thighs, my breasts, and let myself take deep gulping breaths of air. I cannot help but let out a moan of pleasure. I squirm on my sheets as the pleasure slowly subsides. I roll onto my side and fall into a luxurious slumber. And whom shall I dream of? The woman who has kissed me in the woods and has ignored me ever since. The woman whom I cannot stop thinking about. Waking to thoughts of her, I feel a new throbbing come from between my legs and allow myself to reach down once more. And this time as I circle my fingers to draw pleasure, I imagine it is Miss Lister's fingers touching me, her face in front of me, and her lips on mine.

When I wake a short while later, I pray for forgiveness. I do not know what has come over me. How could I possibly have such thoughts – and over a woman? A woman my aunt has warned me against. A woman who seems to have lured and bewitched me. A woman I should never have had anything to do with. I shall not pleasure myself like that again. I have resisted it for so long and in just two weeks since meeting Miss Lister again I have become... of loose morals. I shall need to pray a great deal.

If only I had someone to talk to about such matters. My sister is too far away, and I fear her husband reads her letters. Even if I could speak to her, what would she say? Probably that I should pray for forgiveness for such thoughts and never see Miss Lister again.

After my aunt warned me about getting too close to Miss Lister, I asked Mrs Priestley, a long-standing friend of the Listers what she knew of her. She had only praise to offer and seems to think highly of her, although says she is an 'odd fellow'. It didn't reassure me. I wonder now if she'll tell Miss Lister I was asking after her?

Lord, deliver me from this temptation. I do not deserve any pleasures of the flesh. I have wronged another and deserve no pleasure or comfort in life. I shall devote myself to study and prayer and reside here at Crow Nest with my aunt until my dying day. Who am I to deserve happiness? God will judge me for taking pleasure and my improper thoughts. I hope Miss Lister continues to ignore me, for it will make my task easier. I shall have nothing more to do with Miss Lister of Shibden Hall.

Miss Lister

It only took a week for me to receive a letter from her.

I had stored up all my willpower to ignore the little thing for at least a month, and she crumbles and writes to me after just seven days. I truly have her on a string. Her letter asks if we can meet again and explains that she will happily come accompanied by her aunt if I deem it appropriate. She leaves the choice of whether we are alone or not to me. That suggests she wishes us to be alone but does not want to presume. How sweet of her.

I wonder what thoughts are flying through her head now? I wonder if she can even imagine what is beyond kissing? She seems so innocent, I doubt her hand has ever even explored her own body, let alone another's. Mrs Priestley tells me she has been proposed to over the years but never been seen with anyone. Poor thing, I would have assumed she had not even been kissed before, except that how she kisses me suggests otherwise. It seems that young Miss Walker has had more experience than she lets on. I imagine she prays for forgiveness after every impure thought!

As I think on her now and record her letter in my diary, as I record all I write and receive, I feel as though I have been rather mean in my estimation of her. Perhaps she isn't half so unintelligent as I believed. She rises to my conversation and although she appears lacking in education, she does seem to have the capacity for it. I could suggest a few books to her and once she has read them, I could question her and see what she makes of them. That would give me a good measure of whether she has the capacity to learn in order for her to be suitable companion to me. I should hate for her to be interested only in gossip rather than history and philosophy.

I wonder too what her experience of relations is? She may well have secrets – I've hidden mine well. I wonder what Miss Walker has been up to in her time? She is attractive and must surely have the same urges as I do. As I write about her in my diary, I feel myself getting warm down below and know that tonight I shall take pleasure while thinking of her. I wonder if she would ever even dream of doing the same with thoughts of me?

I decide to make her wait. I write back to say I'd be happy to visit her and her aunt but am busy until next Tuesday. Five days for her to think about me or forget me. I shall meet with her and her aunt, and if she seems interested I shall offer to take her for a short walk.

I think I shall need to progress past kissing quite soon before my interest wanes. I am not as young as I was and do not wish to exhaust too much of my time working on her only for her to reject me at the final stage. I need to be sure quite soon that she is of the same mind as me, that she too has feelings only for the fairer sex, and, ideally, only for me.

Without meaning to, I allow myself to picture us here together at Shibden Hall. Half my daydreams allow pessimism to creep in and I imagine her annoying me with not wanting to walk or socialise and not standing up for herself, and I imagine us falling out and me sending her back to her home of Crow Nest. The other half of my thoughts see us in contentment, living side by side, going for walks, tending to the estate, drawing up plans for more renovations and improvements and retiring to our bedroom together where she allows me to pleasure her.

It dawns on me suddenly that Miss Walker is a very wealthy heiress with a considerable sum at her disposal, one which far overshadows my own income. If she would love me and live with me here at Shibden, I may be able to avail myself of some of her wealth.

It is a selfish, shallow thought, but once thought, I cannot unthink it. Suddenly wooing Miss Walker becomes more than just seeking pleasure and companionship. Wooing Miss Walker could also result in my financial benefit. I could finish my grand plans for the Hall. Moreover, what I have wanted to do for several years, but not had the means to do, is travel farther afield, beyond Paris, beyond Europe. Winning Miss Walker would mean I have the finances to travel and do it in more luxury than ever before.

I write to her again and say I am now suddenly free on Saturday to visit her at Crow Nest if it is not too soon and she is available. I wager she will be.

Miss Walker

Three different relatives have written to me now whom I've not heard from for months. Now suddenly they all appear, concerned for my welfare. News of my new friendship with Miss Lister has travelled fast; yet their warnings only add to my feelings that I wish to see her, and I care ever less for what anyone else thinks. I admire that Miss Lister seems so unabashed by what people say. I shall endeavour to be more like her. What reputation is it that I have to lose by my acquaintance with her? I do not believe I even have a reputation, so little have I been involved in the world. I should like to have more of a reputation; whether it be good or bad, at least I should have one. Let me be the talk of the family, the church, the town and all of Yorkshire!

I believe I am past my final opportunity of marriage to a man, so what damage can a friendship with an 'odd fellow' like Miss Lister do? I shall become an 'odd fellow' too.

No sooner do I have bold thoughts like these than my doubts come to the fore. Why must I always be in two minds? From what to wear and what to sew; from whom to see and what to write in letters. I believe I must have never been allowed to make a decision and consequently, when thrust to make them since my parents died, I doubt my own ability to decide even the smallest things. Perhaps I should start small. I should try and practise making decisions on small matters. Perhaps assert my authority in the house more, rather than let my aunt do it. It is my house, after all.

I wonder how Miss Lister manages to run her own estate? She even collects the rents herself sometimes and all the tenants know her. I heard she negotiates herself over the coal mines on her land. I have coal mines on my estate, but they seem to be managed without my interference. Perhaps I should take an interest? I might pay a visit to one and see for myself. That would be a shock to the men – little me, turning up in my pink ribboned bonnet to say good morning. I see why Miss Lister dresses all in black. Although it must be striking for the men to see a woman amongst them, she does not stand out quite as much as I do. I look down at my dainty hands and my feet in embroidered slippers. Perhaps I am not made for coal mines, but I shall endeavour to find out more about my own estate. I shall ask for the finances to be brought to me. I probably will not be able to understand them, but it is high time I took an interest. As my family of money-seekers circle around me, it may be in my interest to know what is at stake.

Chapter Three

Summer, 1832: A ponderance of futures as neighbouring heiresses

Miss Lister

This time all she talks about is marriage and family. We sit apart, despite our prior passionate kisses. It is as though her aunt or mine is watching us, even though we are alone. Marian returns from a visit and joins us, removing any chance of another kiss, and I find myself leaving them to their small talk as my mind wanders to more pleasurable things.

Marriage indeed. I thought better of her.

I believe Father always knew I would never marry a man; I find them repugnant. I am happy in the company of a few, such as my late uncle who allowed me to stay here at Shibden Hall when I was younger, and my beloved brother Samuel, who was so cruelly snatched from us. I can entertain an intelligent man, but most of them have wandering eyes and hands and are driven by just one thing, surrounded by their own self-worth, always looking down their nose at others, especially women. They believe women are to be impressed and conquered, whilst inside us all is the same mind and intelligence. Men, though, are governed by their bodies and what power they can attain over others through money and position. They claim women as their wives and preside over them and their unfortunate children, whilst they are unanswerable to anyone but themselves and God, who seems to allow them to act as they please.

I am envious of men's freedoms to do as they please but do not wish to be one. I wonder if they are all as frustrated as the women they marry? Perhaps no one has pleasure with one another, excepting what is necessary to procreate. I wonder, are there only a few of us who have any pleasures of the flesh at all? I've met women older than me who have never even touched themselves. No one tells us what pleasure is so freely available; it remains instead a secret we may only learn by accident. It is male pleasure we are informed about, male pleasure that is gossiped about and focussed on, as though women are merely vessels for childbirth. If it were spoken of more and we were all happily pleasuring ourselves, what need would we have of men? I have heard from others who have lain with men that it is quick and uncomfortable. Although we are supposed to fit together as God intended, He also generously gifted us with an ability to not need the other for pleasure. Yet women risk a child, out of wedlock even, for quick pleasure which could be attained alone or with another woman with no threat of a child, and without having to endure male company. It is not the forbidden fruit, for it serves no evil.

If God made me, He must intend me to be as I am. If so, can He judge me for how I behave, when I did not choose this form? I did not ask for a heart that loves only women. How can it be a sin to pursue how I feel, when He made me feel this way? These thoughts are not new. With each relationship they resurface. Questioning. I wonder what Miss Walker thinks of all this. Or is she entirely innocent and virtuous?

Miss Walker

As her eyes bore into me, all I can think is that I must look pretty. All I can think to talk about is family trifles and then I stupidly bring up marriage. Thankfully Marian joins us; she is oblivious to our stolen kisses and my thoughts that race and race and make me sound stupid. At least I manage to remain looking pretty.

Father told me to be pretty. That was all he ever said. He never said I *was* pretty – just that I should look it. That way, he said, I would be chosen. The pretty girls are chosen. I wasn't entirely sure what I would be chosen for, or if I ever would be, but the way he said it made it sound important. My maids said it too – this will make you look pretty, they'd say, as they tore through my hair with a comb. This will make you look pretty, they'd say, as they tightened my corsets. This will make you look pretty, my mother would say, as she had me fitted for a new dress.

I was never sure if looking pretty was worth it.

Miss Lister

Miss Walker is naturally very pretty and makes me feel less so in her presence. Look pretty my dear, Mother would bark at me and at poor unpretty Marian. As if saying it would make us so. Luckily, she gave up on that quickly. Then it was, do not be too intelligent or people will not like you. Why does a girl need to study, Jeremy, why do we need to send our daughter to school? She quickly changed her mind when Father said I would be out of sight, out of mind. He winked at me as he said it. The annoying old fool was right though: being out of

25

the sight and mind of my mother was the best thing that could have happened to me.

I knew from a young age that I was more intelligent than her and I believe she knew it too. I kept her at arm's length, answered dutifully and 'looked pretty' as best I could. Arguing only ever resulted in being sent to my room, so I just stayed there. Marian was no help. She was Mamma's little girl. She at least tried to look pretty, though she was far from it. She made an effort to be graceful, to play the piano and sew. I did these too but always with an air of resentment as I would have rather been outside with Father or out riding with Samuel when he was home, or alone reading a book. Anything but making small talk and being told to push my shoulders back, or what colours would suit me best.

I never envied my mother having myself as a child. I was precocious and probably very annoying – but all they had to do to be rid of me was send me to school like Samuel. Then one day when I was fourteen, with a wink, Father made it happen. It was Father who allowed me to walk with him, ride with him, shoot with him – but always in secret. I liked the freedoms he afforded me and that he respected my desires, but he was not a clever man either. I believe he thought of himself as my saviour, when I was merely biding my time to be rid of him. Them. All of them. My mother, father, Marian, Market Weighton and all its simpleness. School was an adventure and it was there I would finally meet someone my own age who was not 'pretty' either, but free and wild like me.

Eliza was exciting. I had thought I had been an awkward child, but her parents must have been run ragged. She objected to everything and had been sent to school to teach her some manners through brute force, for nothing else seemed to affect her. I had been cheeky to my parents and frustrated them, but

Eliza worried hers. She worried me. She was not pretty, but she was beautiful in my eyes. She was the first person to kiss me. I didn't care that one day she would ignore me and the next sneak into my bed. I didn't care that she made wild plans for our futures but then dismissed me as below her, or too plain.

She had me on a string, but I didn't mind. She taught me to kiss. Made me realise that girls could kiss girls. That I was not alone in how I felt.

She was locked away in an asylum.

Afterwards, I looked back upon our letters and wondered if I should have seen that her wildness was madness, that her passion was insanity. I feared that the only women that felt like I did would all be mad, or that I too was mad. I reassured myself that the letters were just letters between young girls in and out of love with each other. I reassured myself that the next person I loved would be better for me. Would love me back equally. Would not go insane.

I look across at Miss Walker as she giggles with Marian, the two of them without a care in the world.

When I was young, I believed that if I wished enough, I would wake up a boy. Not because I wanted that form, but I wanted all the privilege it allowed. I would never have had any worries about my future had I been the eldest boy. My inheritance would have been set and the world would have been mine. I would have chosen a wife for love and would have been proud to have been seen with her. Instead, because of my form, not my mind or myself, I was condemned to wait on others to bequeath me money, such as the generous allowance my uncle gave me when I moved in with him and my aunt all those years ago. I finally had my own purse!

For many years, while dear Sam was alive, I believed I would still have to marry. I suppose little Marian felt the same, and still does. Now she is beholden to me as the eldest and my choices, and although she threatens to marry the first man who will have her and have a baby boy to strip me of the Lister inheritance, she seems also to be without the desire to be enamoured with a man. Perhaps she is just too shy. Or does she feel as I do? She has never suggested it. Is she perhaps just too afraid and so will remain a spinster, unsatisfied by the world yet unwilling to go out and claim some of it for herself?

Miss Walker

If we were men we would go out for a ride or shoot and have something to discuss, instead of making small talk. My back aches from the effort of maintaining my posture and my corset digs in. Now she talks with Marian and I have a moment to look back at her; her dark hair, dark clothes, her own posture which seems so much stronger than mine. Looking at her reminds me of watching my brother playing with a sword and swaggering around with his shotgun and dogs. I wanted to look like him. John was not pretty, but attractive, fun. He never had to sit with his knees together, or sew, or play the piano. I had the piano keys before me but it never sounded the way I wanted it to. I was trying to make beautiful music but all you could hear was the 'try'. I'm not sure if I was jealous of him or the way he was treated. Probably both. But he was my friend, my confidant. He would protect us as Father did, even if he teased me and made me giggle at the table when we shouldn't. John knew that my job was to look pretty, and his job was to one day inherit and manage the Walker estate and protect me.

I knew nothing of boys, except that one day one would choose me, and I would be loved. I wish I could go back to my younger self – but what would I say? Would I tell her of what is to come? Could I offer anything of reassurance? As even now in adulthood I am as torn and as fragile as my childhood self. Born into privilege yet made to suffer for it. I know I am blessed in many ways, but to be left alone in this world so young seems too cruel. My parents were the constant in my life. While John went off to school and adventures, the family home always contained Elizabeth and me, my mother and father. They were happy days of trying to play the piano and paint and learn languages, none of which I was any good at but none of which mattered. I was loved. I was safe. I would one day be chosen, which I rather feared and hoped would not happen.

My world was dashed apart when my parents died within months of each other, leaving myself and Elizabeth to mourn and fear for our futures. But we had John to protect us. John, who strode about with swords and purpose and who could play a tune on the piano with great gusto. He would manage the estate and, in turn, us. He would make sure that if someone did choose us, they would be the right person, a good sort of man who would treasure us and not take us too far from our home.

John and I both warned Elizabeth not to accept that bastard of a man, but she ignored us, despite John's protestations that he could look after us. She no doubt feared that having two dependent spinster sisters would put off any potential wife for John and jeopardise his chances at happiness. Captain Sutherland took her away from us, all the way up to Scotland, and never loves her as she deserves.

John did find a loving wife not long after, but God decided to take John from us all. It was just two years past, on his honeymoon of all times. He died and left his new wife alone with child, which she lost too, and the Walkers did nothing to provide for her, but cast her aside as if she and John had never existed.

And now I am alone; but Miss Lister has entered my life and may offer me a different path of comfort and protection. With her as a neighbouring companion, I would be able to stay where I know, where the people are familiar, with my memories surrounding me. And I believe she offers something else too, something I have only glimpsed and been denied: pleasure. A blush rises to my cheeks and I am sure she sees it. She stands abruptly and takes me for a walk; she does not invite Marian, and I am whisked away into the woodlands and our mouths find each other once more.

To be held by her makes me feel so alive; more would be to burst. I look into her face and she seems earnest. I never want it to end, but she turns us back towards home and we carry on with our walking as if we had never stopped. Before long we are back at the Hall and she is bundling me into my carriage and I am hot and flushed and know not what to say other than a meek goodbye, and please call on me soon.

I try not to think about the gossip I have heard about Miss Lister. Now that I know her, I shall make up my own mind. Admittedly, I now know well that something I heard is true: she certainly will never marry a man.

I believe I have been luckless in love. I assumed I would be chosen, as I was taught I would be. That I would not have to worry about it, or actively pursue. I never imagined that I would reach this age and be a spinster. I will be thirty years old next year. I am probably past having children now, or would struggle to have them. My body feels older. Small lines corner my eyes and remain visible across my forehead, which will only deepen in time. I'm tired more often, my back aches all the time and I am always between a headache or soreness in my throat or a cough I cannot shake off. I no longer feel as I did even just a few years ago. I was still filled with hope, and even after what happened... I still believed I stood a chance at happiness. But then God chose to pluck my one chance of a good marriage away from me too... and I am questioning my own sanity for having feelings about another woman.

Oh, if only she were a man, I would not hesitate. I would have begged her to propose, probably after our first meeting. I would have had no doubt in my mind that I could spend the rest of my life with her, share all I have with her. It would have been a perfect match. She has her own money so would not be desperate for mine, though I'd happily share it. We already have some of the same friends, so I would not have to move far, if at all. I would not be dragged up to Scotland like my poor sister, plucked from all she ever knew to be with *him*. Oh God, how can You be so cruel to snatch one suitor away from me and then place another before me, even more perfect, only for it to be disallowed? Not legally I suppose, but morally and in Your eyes. Is it a test? Do You tease me with her? Am I being punished? Is my whole life to be tormented?

Miss Lister, how I wish you were a man. I would marry you this instant.

Or is it because you are not a man that I have fallen for you? Is that wrong? That when I think of you, I think of your soft lips, your female form... Oh, I am wicked and must pray for forgiveness.

Miss Lister

She kisses well; I am sure she has done so before. She must have at least some experience, though it surely cannot compare with my own.

With Miss Walker packed off home again, Marian seems very interested in my new friend. We talk for a while in easy company as sisters should, but we always end up riling each other. I do not know what starts the argument, but she marches off and I am left wishing our brother Samuel were here, the three of us again. School gave me the independence and educational start I needed, and returning home again just made me want to leave. Mother, Father, Marian. The only joy was when Samuel came home, but then he joined the Army. He left us for Ireland and would never return. He drowned, the letter said. No details. An accident.

He had been a strong swimmer.

We had written to each other always. I'd shared everything with him. I was angry for years that he would be foolish enough to get himself drowned and leave me. I was now the eldest of our Lister clan; with just Marian and I surviving of the six of us, and all our mother would say was, look pretty or neither of you will be chosen.

Without my brother, I was now at the mercy of my uncle who sat on the bulk of the Lister estate and incomes. Father had little left and didn't seem to be of even the slightest ill heath, excepting his elbow injury from the American War, in which anyone would think he'd lost an arm. Luckily my uncle knew me well and how unlikely I was to marry. I would need my own income to survive in this world and I am grateful to this day that he knew it. He understood my desire for independence; he himself had never married and nor had my aunt, with whom he always lived at Shibden. Brother and sister together, as I had long hoped dear Sam and I would be in time. We'd have had a jolly time together at Shibden like our uncle and aunt.

After years of visiting, I finally moved into Shibden in my twenties to escape from my parents. Despite a generous allowance from my uncle, it was only when I was thirty-five years old that I finally gained my own income when my uncle passed. He had chosen to divide the estate and incomes between myself, my father and my aunt, which I understood, although couldn't help begrudging. My aunt had never had much involvement in the estate, excepting the running of the Hall and its staff, and Father had so little interest in anything but reading the newspaper, they were both quite happy for me to take it all on myself, which was no easy task. While my uncles and father and their predecessors had never run up any debt, neither had they managed to profit. They were happy to live off the rents and so never had any involvement with the profitable wool trade or any new industry. In fact, they retreated from public life and revelled in the seclusion Shibden affords.

It was hard work and of course I met with objection each step of the way. Folks are reluctant to change, especially changes which cost, and they certainly didn't want to deal with a woman. They are more used to me now and although I see only a third of the profits, I feel as though the estate is mine. I just wish I had more income to invest. My other uncle's property, Northgate House, sits empty in town but has such potential. I see it becoming a first-rate hotel, possibly with a dance hall. One day I might get my hands on that too.

Then to poor Marian goes an annual amount, but my uncle must have assumed that she would marry, or that I would be responsible for her. Of course, I'd never cast her out, but she could go back to our mother's house in Market Weighton if she wished. She seems intent on staying here with us though, even though she moans about us all, and about Shibden. I wonder if she is lonely? I expect every time we come to blows, even over the most trivial thing, that she will pack her bags and return to her friends back home. But she does not. She is attached to my aunt, as we all are, and perhaps she thinks she has more chance of a suitor in Halifax.

Miss Walker

There are no suitors in Halifax. They have all been suggested and paraded before my sister and me, and we before them. Not one of them turned our eye. They all had a back story of debt or misdemeanours. Not one of them ever asked about us and what we wanted from life; they merely gushed over what they could offer us, as if they were the ones sitting on a fortune.

Then Sutherland strode in and my sister's knees went weak. I could see why, but I could also see through it. I never trusted him but couldn't put my finger on the reason why, at least not until it was too late. She was smitten by the Captain who swaggered and pomped and probably could have done better than my sister for his looks but would have only managed a clergyman's daughter for his lack of money and standing. He'd achieved his Captaincy but that was all. He was penniless but good with words, full of charm and dashing. My sister didn't stand a chance.

Then there were the other men, the ones already married who still believed they could win over another woman. There have been a number of them. We should perhaps not let them into the house at all. Women only, like the men do in their clubs.

They have their 'men only' places but we are not permitted any. Any man can stride into our houses, our rooms even, and make themselves at home. Say crude things and even lay their hands on us, as if in innocence, but in truth they are guilty. It's the married ones you must watch, especially when you see a plain wife with an attractive man. He's married her for money, and therefore she will never satisfy him. I suppose the same is true for attractive women with ugly husbands. I see their eyes and hands wander, to gently touch what has been forbidden to them; an attractive partner. Or perhaps everyone is having affairs and committing adultery in the plain sight of God and no one speaks of it? Perhaps I am so separate from this world and so naive that I have no real idea of what goes on at all. We can only go by our own experiences and what we hear. If all the gossip I hear is true, and that's only what has been found out, then all people are wicked.

Miss Lister

Father paid for a woman to visit me when I was still young and not yet aware of my own body. Father had no money to give me an allowance like my uncle did, but he did pay for this woman to come to my room.

She was of average beauty but of fine body. She said that she was mine for the evening and she asked me what I wanted to do with her. I had no idea. It was like putting a piano before someone who cannot play. I liked how she looked but had no idea how to make the keys sing. Luckily, she was kind and took her time with me. She kissed me first, long and hard. I'd kissed Eliza before, but this was something forbidden and so was even more enticing. It wasn't the soft, gentle, uncertain kisses of girls but a woman who had kissed many others. She held my arms and then my neck and back and her tongue made its way into my mouth, a first for me, but ravishing. I resisted at first; it felt too intimate, an invasion of my space, but after a while I opened wider to let her in. She carried on, kissing and kissing, wide mouthed, tongue searching, teeth clashing occasionally, but she never pulled back. All my world narrowed. Drawing back for air and pressing in again with lips and tongues, hands grasping at arms, shoulders, waist, neck and up into her hair, pulling her to me, as if I had been let loose and never wanted her to be apart from me.

She held my lip gently between her teeth and I searched for hers, holding it then releasing, then sucking, then more deep, powerful kisses as our mouths moved together, unsure where mine ended and hers began. Then she moved away from my mouth's reach and kissed my neck and shoulders, pushing down my dress and she was at my ear lobe, sucking gently and tickling with her tongue and then back to my neck, nipping and kissing, soft then hard. She pulled me to the bed, sat behind me and undid my dress and corset, all the while teasing my neck with her lips, as my heart raced. My dress fell to the floor and she pulled me back onto her lap and kissed me again on the mouth as she pulled out my curls. I felt vulnerable and would have preferred for it to have been the other way around, but I hadn't known how to do what she was doing. I was learning, I was her pupil. This would be what I would desire to do to others.

Her hands reached for my breasts which had never been truly touched before, not by determined hands like these. She pushed me down and kissed my naked breasts, my sides, my stomach, and squeezed my thighs. I felt so alive and yet afraid that it would end. I lay still, allowing her to touch me all over with her hands, her lips, her tongue, my body growing hot and out of control as she moved down the bed and before I could move or protest she leaned in and her mouth found my queer and she kissed it and licked it gently and then began to lick harder and seemed to suck on me, focusing all my pleasure into that one spot, which I had discovered myself before, but had never known could be so alive. As I lay there at this woman's mercy, learning what pleasures my body could give me, and what I could do to elicit this pleasure from others, I wondered what else there could be in the world as satisfying as giving oneself to another... but then I could think no more as she worked me to a state that people never speak of: consumed by pleasure and so alive and then in a wave of pleasure emanating out to my toes and fingertips, I knew that this was what I wanted. Not with an unfamiliar woman paid for by Father, but from a woman who loved me, whom I would love and care for and give pleasure to. I knew I wanted to make women's bodies sing. I committed to learning to read the music and play the notes.

In the way that I am, after all that pleasure, I sat back in bed with my new tutor and got out my pocketbook and pen. I asked questions and she showed me with her hands how to elicit pleasure with fingers and circles, and pinches and tickles and squeezes and how women's bodies, unlike men's she told me, can be aroused from anywhere. Even just kissing an earlobe can drive a woman to pleasure. I made notes, which somewhat surprised her, and tried a few things on her. I liked to draw pleasure and to be on top looking down, clutching her wrists in my hands as I pressed my mouth to her breasts and neck and down to her queer. A discovery itself of a fascinating space, which looks unwelcoming but is easily opened and explored and swells with passion which you can see rising in a flush across her chest and neck and face as she loses herself to you. Women's bodies have fascinated me ever since; so different from each other, each one a new discovery.

I think I was her best pupil.

I have never seen a man's body unclothed, at least not alive; nor do I wish to. I'm not sure what their down-there is all about. God must have been in a hurry at that part. Sometimes I can appreciate the beauty in their faces and understand why a weaker woman may like a broad-shouldered man, but their hands are rough and ungraceful, their faces sharp with stubble, their hips narrow and bottoms flat. Their ugly Adam's apples bob up and down as they speak, a reminder of their maleness. Their voices are gruff and they lack softness in any aspect. I better not start on their egos...

Women are the fairer sex and although I am one of them, I believe I stand apart. I have a soft body and breasts and a queer like them, but I also know how to pleasure them more than any man. For men, I learned, can only have pleasure once, then they need to recover. We women are blessed with a never-ending capacity for pleasure, and a variety of it.

Poor fellows. Little do they know what they are missing.

Chapter Four

Summer, 1832: Difficulty in finding private time to be alone at Shibden

Miss Lister

We continue with our now weekly meetings but unfortunately Marian and my aunt like Miss Walker too, so often it's a family affair in which even my father joins, so it becomes the four of us Listers with her until I am occasionally able to steal her away just for myself. I encourage Miss Walker to read and learn as I do, but Marian shows keenness and I become a tutor to them both. Even Aunt and Father listen in as they pretend to sew and read the newspaper respectively, as I share my books and notes from the science lectures I attended in Paris.

I am enjoying these visits and family time and do not feel in such a hurry to go travelling again as I had when I first arrived. I wonder if domesticity and family life has me in its clutches already.

As I write up my diary for the day from the notes in my pocketbook after another visit from Miss Walker, I ponder why they all seem surprised at my desire to learn. How do they find contentment here? If only I could quieten my mind sometimes. Allow myself to just sit, as others do. Instead it needs feeding with information; it is never satisfied. Each new topic or theory leads to another and a lifetime is not long enough to read even the smallest amount of what has been written. The task seems unmanageable, so I try to focus on particular themes; mathematics, physiology, histories, languages. Then I will get taken up with music or landscape gardening or bird watching or politics. How easily I become obsessed! I was lucky that Father saw it in me when I was young and sent me to school. I was the brightest student, but it quickly became dull and I asked too many questions that the teachers could not answer. I grew restless and troublesome. Even now, I continue to read and better myself with knowledge but often I ask, to what end? Whilst I may be more privileged than most women of our generation, we are all still barred from franchise, the law, medicine and religion: all the foundations of our nation.

My assertions and emotions, whilst natural to any man, in female form are deemed improper. Displaying our intelligence is threatening, our free spirit is a lost soul, our physicality is unladylike, our singleness is unholy, our loneliness and anxiety manifest as madness, and our frustrations and our anger mark us out as women to be locked away; poor victims to the female malady.

Paris is far more free-thinking and forward-looking. My most recent sojourn there lasted for nearly two years, my aunt visiting with me for some of the time. It was always a glorious time of new friends and experiences, good food and parties, conversations that enthralled me and an opportunity not afforded to me in England: I wrote to ask for permission to attend lectures on science and to my own surprise was granted permission to attend, at least to sit at the very back where no one would see me. Not officially, but I was not forbidden.

Anatomy was my favourite subject. The body fascinates me; each part a miracle but so fragile and susceptible to damage and disease. Perfect yet imperfect, and here were human beings trying to fix bodies that had broken, make them work again, cure them, improve them, edging in on God's work. I was fascinated. I tell Miss Walker and Marian of the bodies I have seen and they are repulsed but enthralled.

To see a corpse makes one feel more alive, I believe, and in some way, more detached from one's own body. It is just a vessel. A marvellous but flawed vessel whose appearance we cannot choose. Our bodies do not reflect us, but may limit us, or set us free. They are how people see us and judge us, dictating our life's course regardless of the soul inside. To see one cut open, the raw flesh and muscles and tissues and veins, I watched on in wonder. Had I been a man, I would have been a doctor. Probably not the most sympathetic doctor as I find many people infuriating, but I would have worked on research at the forefront of science. They believe they can re-animate a body! I should like to see that.

Here in Yorkshire, the world closes in and I am absorbed with what women usually focus on – finding a partner – and this neighbouring heiress Miss Walker is now a viable choice. After suffering pleasantries with the family yet again, she suggests we go for a walk, and I know well what she means. More kissing in the woods or can we finally move to something more? If only we had a private place away from our houses and families. What would be the chances of finding a lover just on the border of my own estate, who has been there all along? She is in my mind ever more and I can tell I have infected hers, but my previous loves come back to haunt me and make me wary. Can I really love again, or trust another with my heart?

After poor Eliza was taken from me and I met Isabella, I had hoped that she would be the one for me. She certainly felt the same as me about women and we did have some fun, but she was never enough for me. I feel cruel for it, but she was not clever enough. Though she pleasured me well and could be good company, I knew I needed more to spend my entire life with someone. I loved her home at Langton Hall, perfectly situated just seventeen miles from York, and we could have lived between our two homes; her sister, brother and mother were all good company too. Her brother was the same age as me and we got along well. His wife died a few years ago, but he now seems content to come and go with his son Thomas, the next to inherit, leaving a female household of three women, none of them with any inclination to marry. But I did not choose her. I chose Mariana, who was never meant to be mine.

I look back through my old diaries and re-visit my younger self. It was always Mariana for me. From the moment we met in York everything about her excited me, and for a long time I believed the same was true for her. All those years ago, an exchange of vows, our futures were settled together and then she received a proposal from an old fool of a man with a large amount of land in Cheshire.

He will die soon, she would tell me, and we will be set for life. I was left waiting in the wings for my time to perform, which never came. Waiting, awfully, for him to die. But the old fool has too much life left and instead seems to drain it from Mariana. She is no longer the woman I loved, would have given anything for, spent my every living day with. She took a gamble on him, his life, and lost. It was a gamble I never wanted her to take. In the end we both lost.

After Mariana married, I spent more and more time abroad or visiting other friends, not wanting to return to the family at Shibden alone. Then it was Maria whom I met in Paris who took my heart and we formed an idea of a future together, but she too was unable to satisfy me. I grew cold towards her and by the time I left her in Paris, just before my uncle passed away and I received some inheritance, I was done with her and have never been in contact again. Foolishly, as I see now, I was still confident in my early thirties that the perfect woman for me would arrive. But here I am past forty, alone again.

Miss Walker

She tells me she has dissected a head! I have so many questions I daren't ask her in front of her family; was it horrible, were you afraid it would come alive, do you think God thinks that's a proper thing to do? In the two years she most recently resided in Paris, I sat at home. Sewing. Possibly doing a few sketches. I may have read one or two novels. Oh, how different our lives are. I am jealous, of course, though I would never be one for dissection. Her world is much wider than mine. Though my family have more wealth (better to never say that aloud to her!), she seems to have had more privilege. Her father sent her away to school, encouraged her to travel, paid for tutors. Confidence emanates from her. How could she ever be satisfied by me?

I must think on my own accomplishments.

Nothing comes to me. I look good in bonnets. Oh, how shallow I am. I am nothing more than a vessel for clothing and pleasantries. My sewing is half-hearted; my aunt finishes my endeavours when I grow bored with them. I do not think there's a single handkerchief I can take full credit for.

I am an expert at melancholy! I shall mock myself before others do.

I look pretty. That's sincere. I would venture to say that I am prettier than Miss Lister. Good that I am too, otherwise she'd not look twice at me. I believe she likes how ladylike I am. She praises my posture and delicate hands. She likes to see me sewing and drawing. I shall become more accomplished for her. I shall engage an artist as my tutor. Perhaps I shall take up piano lessons again and surprise her with a recital one day. I shall whisper to her before I start to play that I am not wearing any drawers! That might pique her interest in my playing even more. How saucy I am! I have never felt so base before, but I find my thoughts stray these days. It is her influence on me. My other friends have been far too sedate all these years.

She is cleverer than me though, of that I am certain. Not just in what she has studied, but in her mind. Anyone can read a lot, but you must be clever to digest it and extrapolate meaning to discuss with others. I wonder if she minds my lack of intelligence compared to hers? Does she seek a companion who would be her equal, or just for company? If she represents an intelligent husband, is he content with a milder, but more attractive wife? Perhaps she does not want an equal in intellect, for then they might disagree and argue, always challenging each other, whilst instead I listen and ask her to explain it to me clearly, like the dutiful submissive wife. I shall stick to my novels. Her science seeks to make sense of the world but are novels not another way of doing so, even those dismissed by Miss Lister as a waste of time? I love to hear others' stories and choices and dramas. Relate to heroes and heroines and lose myself in a world unreal. I do not want to know how the brain works, I want to see its workings in art, words, imagination. I want to enjoy the outcome of a mind, not see the components that make it work. I like the face of a clock, not the clockwork.

Miss Lister

I had to shave all the hair off the head as it was crawling with lice.

I do not tell any of them this detail. But when I am alone again, I consult my diaries from the time and re-read my musings on how something so inanimate had once been so animated in life. What is it that causes it to live and where does that 'life' go upon death? Is that the soul? Why didn't God explain it clearly? In the Bible there are few mentions of anatomy and how we work. Man is discovering it for himself. Is God willing in this? Is this God's work, to discover for ourselves what makes us, or is He angry that we dare to question, interfere, play with bodies in the name of science? Was I interfering with someone's soul? Could they rest peacefully with their head separate from their body? Did my actions hurt them in Heaven?

At least she will not be itching from the lice anymore. For it was a female head.

My mind wanders. How do we have such different forms, men and women? Surely it would have been easier for us to be the same and to be able to procreate alone. To leave it to a form that must choose another, different to itself... is that to ensure there are two guardians of a baby? Though that is not always the case. Or should babies be placed in the care of a community and the responsibility shared, with generations of a family all involved? I suppose that is the ideal. How are some babies left alone with not even one person to care for them? How are others born into wealth and ignored by their parents and family?

I shall never have any babies myself. Though it saddens me to be the end of this branch of the Lister line, I do not feel an urge for it. They are sweet enough; I shall visit Vere, my delightful friend

45

and her new baby soon and quite look forward to it. I marvel at how so small and pathetic a creature can grow so large and become a person, with memories and ambitions and intelligence and the capacity to love, yet also the capacity to hate. To ruin lives of those around them, or to improve them.

The similarities are more than the differences between male and female bodies. We have slightly different shapes, better suited for childbearing or for combat, but our feelings, our experiences of sight, sound, taste, smell and touch are the same. Our emotional capacities are the same. I believe our abilities to learn are the same. Do I wish myself male? I am not sure. I like my body and the pleasures it gives me. It feels manageable and my own. How would I ever know any different? Would life have been easier for my mind, as it is, to be in a male body? Yes. But would it have felt like 'me'? I am not sure.

Miss Walker enters my mind again. As always, these days. I think about her form, smaller than my own, more delicate. Lighter skin and hair than mine, more attractive, definitely. Is it wrong to like a form so similar to my own? Mariana was different again. Even more attractive, taller than me, but of the same hue. A kinder reflection of myself than the one I see in a mirror. She was very different to Miss Walker; perhaps that is why I like her. In her I do not see Mariana or myself, but something new, innocent, like a shiny coin which draws the eye.

Miss Walker is more like Vere. I just hope Miss Walker will not be swept off her feet by a man like Vere was. Vere, who I dreamed would be my new Mariana. Vere, who made me flee Paris and return home to Shibden. Vere, who delighted in all things and would tease me and kiss me but always keep me at a distance. Vere, who would bring me into her elaborate world but remind me I was an outsider. She was a good friend and, in truth, I do not think she ever knew she was cruel. She was innocent in her affection and how she spoke. She was innocent when she told me, full of joy, who had proposed. Her innocent excitement as she gushed that she would become Lady Cameron, as if the title alone was all she'd ever dreamed of. More than when I was with Mariana, I had known that day would come. Vere was beautiful, highborn, intelligent, talented, and of course had wanted to be a wife and mother since she was a child. I could not begrudge her that. It was not her fault I had spent so long dreaming, imagining, hoping, praying, that it would be me that could satisfy her. I had known the truth of it all along, and despite doing my best to guard my heart from her, when she told me of her marriage, I lost another piece of it. Now I have lost so many pieces of my heart, I think I have just enough left for one last love, but if it should be broken but once more, I do not think it can ever again be whole.

Miss Walker may well be what I need. My last chance may prove perfect. We have both shared a captivity of sorts and now in adulthood we are free to remain independent. We have different looks but the same desires. I believe and sincerely hope there is a future for us yet.

I do not think she understands my fascination with the head. Perhaps I should not have told them about it; but it was worth it just to see the disgust on Marian's face.

Miss Walker

Miss Lister may not see me as highborn enough for her. She has aristocratic friends, not nouveau riche as she calls us Walkers. I do not imagine that the friends she always gushes about would appreciate my acquaintance. I'm not sure how they even tolerate

47

Miss Lister's, but at least she has some heritage and education. She probably provides better company than I ever could.

Perhaps she is attracted by my money? Is that part of my appeal? Perhaps she is no better than a money-seeking male suitor. She will lure me in with her charms and embraces and then have me sign a document and she will move into Crow Nest and I will be helpless to stop her.

Perhaps I judge too unfairly. She cannot be as cruel as a man, surely?

Perhaps she will love me because I am so different from her. I think about how we could be long-term companions to each other. Ward off any suitors, or all men altogether, and hide ourselves away at Crow Nest. My heart seems taken with Miss Lister.

I wonder how many relationships she has really had, how many broken hearts she has left in her wake. She is older than me, worldlier, more experienced in so many things, but regardless of our age, backgrounds, dreams and fears, when we are together and our mouths touch and we push ourselves against each other, we are no longer ruled by our minds but by our hearts which beat as one. Is she truly my last chance for happiness?

Chapter Five

Autumn, 1832: A proposal to Miss Walker and the writing of a diary

Miss Lister

Another kiss with Miss Walker. She tells me I am on her mind and I confess that she is on mine too. I record our encounters in my diary, like a confessional that only I can access. To be able to freely expound my innermost thoughts to paper and confine them to a volume to be reflected upon or forgotten and lost to time. I thank God for it. For in my lonely life, it has given me the companion that I long for.

Some days, I almost wish the day to be over before it has begun so I can retire to my small study and write my diary. Writing can give me more pleasure than the day itself sometimes. I find myself undertaking tasks for the reward not of the task itself, but the writing of it.

My first efforts to write a diary ceased after just a few months, but then, remembering the release it gave me, I started again – but life got in the way of writing about it. I'm not sure how the final commitment came about, but from my mid-twenties it was writing into a hardbound volume, bought especially for this purpose, that must have stuck me to my course. I have not missed a day's entry since. I quickly realised how the very act of recording could make even the mundane important. Recording the daily temperature has become somewhat of an obsession. Once you begin to notice something like that, it is very hard to un-notice it. I can tell the temperature now before even looking at the thermometer. A morning test of my own skills, which if correct leaves me feeling quite satisfied.

Now, after so many thousands of entries, I suppose it has become as natural, and as necessary, as sleep itself. I carry a small pocketbook and a watch at all times and look forward to my ritual of writing up my notes on empty pages, recording my daily activities, from the ordinary to the remarkable and folding them inside a bound volume to immortalise my own existence. To what end, I know not. I've tried to understand my own obsession; I know it eases me through my thoughts, allows me to process what I have done, seen, written in letters, said and heard and felt. It is cathartic when times are dull or difficult. But there is more to it than that.

Although it is my voice which echoes onto the page, I am still never sure if it is myself I am writing it for, or some future me, or some other? Another Anne, who listens and sympathises. Or is my idea to share these words? To make some sense of my years of existence to share with others? But what would I edit out, or in? Who would wish to read it, and which parts would they care about? My daily life, my business endeavours, my politics, visiting and writing letters, my health, the daily temperature? I believe it will be something to read back over when my days of activity are done, and I am homebound or worse, bedbound, and my thirst for new knowledge is quenched and I want to remember instead what I have done before.

Do I fancy myself a writer? Could I steal from my own experiences and make a fanciful fiction, or is there enough story from truth in these volumes on my shelf which stare down at me, that little fiction will be required? How many more volumes will I fill with my days?

My diaries may be a way to immortality, like creating buildings to outlive us. But I do not believe that anyone would really care for a woman of Halifax, a place of inconsequentiality which no one has heard of. With no children to pass these volumes to, what will become of my story?

Miss Walker

I have nothing to say for myself. How can she fill pages when I have nothing to write at all? I try to remember what I have done in the day and the blank page stares back at me. Was I awake at all today? Whatever does she write about? It must be very dull. I try again to create something of a list. A very boring list of basic human achievements. Washed. Dressed. Ate breakfast. Read a letter. Should I write what the letter was about? I cannot really remember, just pleasantries from a friend. I barely remember what I replied. Oh God, my letters must be dull if I cannot remember what I wrote just eight hours ago! I must be the dullest friend. No wonder I do not receive many letters. They dread my replies!

I write down what I had for lunch. Did I enjoy it? What do I like to eat? What would I choose to eat if I could have anything? Sponge cake with sweet frost. Oh, why is my life so dull? At least it was, until I met Miss Lister. Anyone who can fill a diary definitely has a more interesting life than me. But I can never write about her for fear someone should read it.

Miss Lister

I write most of my account in plain-hand, to be read by anyone. I have the volumes in my study; they are not hidden, though I doubt any of my family would dare to touch them, let alone read them. They bristle when they see me make a note of something and their eyes roll as I skip upstairs for my time alone with a pen and an empty page to fill. They do not understand my diary writing. My passion. It has become such a part of me. My mind is attuned to remember details, as though viewing my life as an observer ready to record. As events unfold, I am already thinking of how I will explain and describe it in words in my diary, deciding what I will keep and record. Sometimes there are moments which I consciously decide to omit. I edit my diaries in my head, in my pocketbook and in the writing of them. Perhaps I do it to protect my future self, or protect the contents from prying eyes. But then some of my deepest thoughts and sadness I cannot deny from my diary. It seems easier to write of sadness and disappointment; to capture it in words is to lessen the feeling of it, as if shared with a sympathetic friend, whilst the pleasurable times I find myself skipping over in a few lines, as I'm sure I will remember them well without much prompting.

At first, I wanted to record everything factually, but my own voice and feelings crept in and I realised a factual account served no purpose to anyone, least of all myself. I decided I would write everything, painful and personal or otherwise. Of course, to write anything so personal one must be careful about who may see it. So I devised a code, as Eliza and I once had in our letters to each other, and then became so familiar with it that it is as quick to write as plain-hand. The code gives me freedom to write about personal feelings, intimacy, my body and health and my finances, should prying eyes ever peer.

Miss Walker

She will be writing about me! I am in her diary. From the day we first re-met after her latest travels, Miss Lister will have recorded me, described me. I imagine she writes exactly what she thinks. Does she think me plain? Shy? Dull? I must become more interesting! I must seem so boring compared to her.

What I wouldn't give to read of one of her diaries! She tells me any personal information is in code. From what I saw when she gave me a glimpse of them in her study, her handwriting is nearly as illegible as any code.

Everyone knows she writes one. You do not want to get on the wrong side of Miss Lister or she'll immortalise you in her diary. She's known for her pocketbook and pocket watch. People talk as if it is very strange, but I think it is admirable to record everything. An unusual hobby, but writing things down somehow makes them seem important. I should write one too. I start my list again. From lunch onwards. Sat with Aunt. Stroked the dog. Had some tea.

Dear God, is that all I did for the entire afternoon? What wasted hours. What a well stroked dog. He will not like me writing a diary if it starts to occupy more of my stroking time. Perhaps that's why she started it, to fill up some time, to have an excuse to retire early to write it up each evening. Perhaps she never writes it up at all. Perhaps most of the volumes she showed me are empty and it is all a lie. She scribbles things down to create an illusion, so that everyone fears to be recorded, and then she retires early and just stares out of the window, or strokes her dog, knowing she has gained some peace and quiet under a lie that she has maintained for her entire adult life!

Of course she writes a diary. I'm just jealous because I do not have the patience to do it myself.

Perhaps I should stick to painting. That will be my legacy. But my pictures are not very good. They never look how I intend them to and mostly end up on the fire.

Never mind writing my own diary. I will find a way to read hers. Will she ever let me? But do I really want to read what she has written about me? As though being confronted with oneself in the mirror and unable to look away, but worse, you are seen through someone else's eyes who may not be as forgiving. The desire to read them now starts to burn in me. Miss Lister and her precious diaries. I'll read them one day. I'll make sure of it.

Miss Lister

I write about Miss Walker in code. I write about our walks in the woods and kissing in the shelter of the trees away from prying eyes. I write how she lets me hold her and she seems willing and never wants to leave.

I have spent my life trying to hide my relationships with women and make sense of who I am. Who would not think ill of me if they read the truth of my heart? By all means, they may know of my endeavours and travels, but of my heart? What would a reader think to my exclamations of love? My marriage ceremony with Mariana all those years ago? Would they malign me as a miscreant and judge me as they do men who prefer their own sex? Would the dark shame I have lived in fear of fall over my life, my home, my family and tarnish the Lister name? Will my story be erased because of my heart's will to love only women?

This fear is what created my code; it protects me and those I have loved from the ill-will of those who could never understand.

My obsession continues, and I cannot sleep until at least my pocketbook is full of the day's account, and after too many days I feel anxious if I have not written up into my permanent record, which seems to verify my very existence. For if I have not recorded what happened, did it happen at all? If I do not find time one day to edit the volumes myself, whose hands may they fall into?

I showed Miss Walker my diaries and she was in awe. She asked if I'd written about her and I told her I write about *everything*. I reassured her that it was written in a code that only I know, and that our secrets are safe.

Miss Walker

I recognise the handwriting before I open it. I almost daren't, but I must deal with this now or I will not be able to concentrate for the rest of the day. What does she want now? Some friends always want something. Never just to enquire, or send love and warm wishes.

Miss Whitaker wants to travel. Again. She's always asking. She must be frightfully bored. I imagine that if she is asking me then she has asked everyone else that she knows and been declined. Travelling with her would be a nightmare. Hours, days on end in a carriage with her!

We go back a long way, Miss Whitaker and I, and that is probably why I have kept up my correspondence. It is nice to have people in your life that you can reminisce with, who knew the younger you. The carefree version of the person you have become. We did have fun when we were younger, but as we grew older I saw through her exterior and found her very self-centred. She would make you feel important only to ask to borrow your dress, or suggest she needed matching ribbons but couldn't afford them so you felt obliged to buy her some. She would suggest that she was low on sketching paper and remind you it was her birthday soon, or overstay for supper and be too tired to travel until the following day. I would share with her some music and she would play it better than I and know it.

Now she is asking about a trip to Europe as if the whole thing is for my benefit. She would do me a favour by accompanying me and tearing herself from her busy, unmarried life. I bet she wants to meet a foreign suitor. Someone dashing to pluck her out of North of England obscurity. She seems to think I want to travel, that I am as desperate as she is to find a companion and will happily pay for the endeavour.

I want to write back with a brisk, no. Then I wonder if I could allude to having met someone to set the gossip going. I could use the excuse of my recent bereavement and postpone her for another six months while I recover, or rather am wooed by Miss Lister. How vicious of me! Perhaps a trip abroad would do me some good. Away from family, and grief and, dare I say it, Miss Lister. Could I bear to be apart from her? Perhaps that will help me decide how I feel.

But even thinking of the practicalities of travel makes me feel cold. Just the issue of what to pack makes me panic that I will forget something essential, or be poorly dressed for the weather. At least here it is always cold and windy. I stay indoors when it is too hot or too cold. But when travelling, anything could happen. Perhaps it's uncertainty that makes me nervous; waking up in a strange room, not knowing where things are. I am such a coward.

Sometimes I imagine the sea. I'd like to see it, just for a bit and then be whisked back home by nightfall. Miss Lister has travelled widely. I cannot begin to imagine what it would be like. I have been to the Lakes and to my sister's house in Scotland and hated every minute of it. I am like a fish out of water. I know my home. My servants. The order of my days. Perhaps that's why I could never write a diary; I do not deserve one as my experiences are so unimportant.

What if I were to reply yes? I could perhaps see how far the plans are set. Perhaps Miss Whitaker wrote to me in the knowledge that I would say no. Shall I surprise her? I'll write back and say yes. But not yet; I need to leave time for my grief to pass. I cannot let her think I have not taken adequate time to grieve for my loss. I would be planning my wedding now and sending her an invitation if God had not intervened.

I believe John would have approved of Mr Fraser. He had kind eyes and was not much larger than I. He was not intimidating but seemed as shy as I was when he made the journey to see me. Elizabeth recommended him as being better than most of her husband's acquaintances and very pleasing to look at. Not much wealth but enough to show that he was not desperate for mine. He had managed to reach the same age as me without a wife and seemed to wake up one day and realise that perhaps he should make an effort. Of course, he could have chosen someone ten or fifteen years his junior but my sister, ever on the lookout, sold me to him. Somehow.

I was nervous for weeks, not sure why on Earth I'd agreed to even meet him. There were a few things she told me that made me wonder, made my step skip a little at the thought that this could be it. She told me he had a kind face and was earnest. He had served briefly with Sutherland many years ago as a clerk and then dabbled in printing and travelling, then went home to look after his mother and sister when his father died. He was now in want of a wife. The situation would be to live with him half the time at his home in Scotland, near my sister, which would have been wonderful, and half in Yorkshire, where he could keep an eye on the estate. He was a good businessman, she told me, and again she said that he was kind.

I was relieved on his arrival that he was so pleasing to look at, as well as charming, and yes, very kind. He stayed with my aunt and visited me each day for a week. I was excited to see him and we talked easily of our lives and families. He was not much taller than me and had soft hands that were always clean, and I allowed him to take mine in his as he promised he would treasure me.

I had always been afraid of larger men, looming over me; I would always be at their mercy. Men do not realise we spend our lives afraid of them, for at any moment they could turn on us and snap our necks. Once snared into marriage they can do what they will with us. They seem oblivious to their power and strength, that even the strongest will of a woman cannot match in size and muscle.

He did not drink, which I was much relieved to learn. He told me his father had drunk himself to an early death and so he had never touched a drop of alcohol, for he had never admired his father's qualities when under its influence. I have seen my uncles and cousins drink at gatherings and grow louder and cruder and insult each other and their wives and then beg mercy the next day, after irrevocable damage has been done.

I was an easy win really; he just had to be small, kind and sober. Simple qualities of most women, except for a few callous gossips, but harder to find in men, at least in those that I had seen paraded before me thus far. Only in my father and brother did I see such a kindness that no matter their size, no matter that just one of their hands around your neck could force the life out of you, you felt you could trust them; I have seen it in so few, it sorrows me. Men are a different breed to me. As a cat to a lion, animals the same in their basic needs and wants, but so different in form, temperament and wildness. The most a cat can do is scratch. A lion can tear you limb from limb.

Each day as Mr Fraser visited, I knew I could bring myself to kiss him, hold him, learn the lines of his body and how to please him. I would learn to love him, bear him children and give him all my attention and care. He proposed to me before he left, and I accepted.

My reminiscence is interrupted by a note from Miss Lister asking to meet again and my heart quickens.

Miss Lister

A letter arrives from Mariana, when really it is a reply from Miss Walker I am hoping for; another note asking me to call on her or to tell me she is coming over to visit. I hope she has received mine.

How quickly Mariana fades when I have a new interest. Life has got in the way, the days have wearied us, age progresses and now draws us apart. Mariana and I now have far more days apart than together. Her letters seem shallow, informative, not as they once were. Our letters used to be exciting, begging of each other to confirm our next meeting, exulting that we missed each other and found everyone annoying as no one else could compare. But now as I read her words, she seems distant; an old flame, as they say. She is fading into the background. My life now has a new breadth of possibilities stretching before me, a new companion who may come and live with me here at Shibden, who may travel with me to the farthest corners, who may pleasure me, who may end up where I always envisaged Mariana to be: next to me, nearby, for all time.

I wonder if Mariana can feel herself fading from my life? Will the presence of Miss Walker remove the smoke from her eyes and reveal to her how she feels, that I am her true love, her husband? Has it been too long? Have we hurt each other beyond repair? Or will the thought of truly losing me to another be enough to sway her heart back to mine?

Another visit from Miss Walker and a walk to the woods, another kiss, another secret. She worries that we will be seen. I shall have to build us a private place where we can meet, so she will relax and let me kiss her unhindered. I assure her the legalities referring to men kissing men are far removed from affecting women. Women, particularly single women with no attachments, are free to do as they please.

She lets me kiss her again.

Miss Walker

I live for our walks, our kisses, but a guilt grows in me about a truth she does not know. My engagement.

I received a letter from Mr Fraser only a few days after his proposal to tell me he had fallen from his horse. He told me he would mend soon and looked forward to seeing me and planning our wedding. He wrote to me again to tell me he loved me and not to worry, not to rush to Scotland to see him as I had offered, as he would drive down and collect me as soon as he could. He told me he would take me to meet his mother and sister and that they couldn't wait to meet me.

I thought the next letter would confirm the date of my journey to my new life, to meet my new family, but the letter that arrived was from his sister, who told me with great sorrow that Mr Fraser had died of a fever. He had worsened quickly overnight, though he had seemed to be recovering, and died the next morning. She and her mother were with him. He told them to tell me he was sorry to let me down and he wished me every happiness. They invited me to see them, to attend his funeral with them, but it was too much for me to bear; to have been surrounded by strangers, to meet people who could have been my family, to see what life I could have had if God had been kinder to me.

Because we were only engaged, I was not allowed the same rights as a widow to grieve. Only my aunt, my sister and my friend Mrs Ainsworth even knew. We'd not announced it yet. If we had been married, they would have accepted me as Mrs Fraser, the widow.

Just a few weeks later, my aunt insisted that I accompany her visiting. She wanted to get me out of the house and my misery, a secret misery that only she truly knew of. Although she had not been there for many years, she made us call in on the Listers. Awfully, at meeting Miss Lister, and her kissing me, my mind swayed from grief to joy in such a quick time that I lost myself to it and forgot I should be sad.

Miss Lister does not know of my bereavement; I have never told her. How wicked of me! Perhaps I do not deserve any friends at all.

Chapter Six

Autumn, 1832: A new retreat for hidden encounters at Shibden

Miss Lister

Autumn sets in. Summer has passed in a blur since I secured Miss Walker's kisses. We are now almost daily to-and-fro between our homes and sometimes meeting in between where our lands meet, keeping up our public appearance with tea with my family, her aunt, who slowly seems to be warming to me, and mutual friends like Mrs Priestley, whilst always contriving to be alone. She even came into my bedroom last week and we got to a bit more than kissing, but I must bide my time with her as she never truly relaxes. She seems to close up and fall silent but does not seem to have the words to explain. I believe she is conflicted, as many women are, about what is natural, and despite my reassurances we have not got much further than kisses and fumbling, but I have a solution to that. Unfortunately, as I am not the sole owner of the estate, I had to ask permission.

It had all been fine until my damned father and sister decided to join me. My dear aunt and uncle were quite happy for me to learn the management of the estate, be involved and make my own judgements, which has been rather fortuitous over the years; but upon my uncle's passing and in leaving the Hall and estate between Aunt, Father and myself, he caused us to all cluck about like chickens cooped up under the same roof. While my sister had seemed content living at our late mother's estate in Market Weighton, she too decided to move over and fill up more room in Shibden Hall with her quietness and tutting. While my aunt and uncle always seemed happy with my company and satisfied by my choices of friends and pastimes, my sister seems intent on unnerving me. She asks too many questions and gives too many looks of disapproval which make me, usually so sound in my own judgement, begin to question things and lose strength. Everything is imbued with doubt, from who rents our land and buys our coal, to what I wear and eat.

How do people live like this? Always doubting themselves? I see how they have remained stuck in their ways for so long. Especially my sister: the biggest decision she's made in her life was coming over to stay at Shibden, and daily she harks on about it, even though done with, as if she is still in the process of deciding if it is a good thing or not; as if she is not here, but somehow floating between the two residences, neither enjoying nor missing either as she has not committed to one or the other.

But never mind them; I'm now spending much of my time in my new Moss House with Miss Walker in my arms and my lips on hers.

They all thought me mad to commission a new building in amongst the trees at the bottom of the slope towards the beck, especially as summer was already leaving us for colder times. I told them it was for sketching and reading, and so I could have some peace, and they eventually agreed for the small amount it would cost. I had my permission. What need they know of my real want of privacy?

I commissioned some local workers for a simple structure of wood and clay with some small windows, high enough not to be looked into, a thatched roof, fireplace and a heavy wooden door. I built it for Miss Walker, always worrisome about who will see us. It saves her having to be polite to my family on every visit while we itch to be close. I finally decided to call our new little dwelling the Moss House, as after much deliberation on its name I noticed the beautiful green moss on the trees nearby and I look forward to a time when the little house will be overcome with it too. Rather cleverly it keeps us away from them all, and the prying eyes of servants too. It is ours alone. There is just one key to its door, which I carry upon me.

Little do my family know what goes on in our Moss House. Our secret place that no one else is permitted to enter. No one but I, and the woman of my choosing. Our private sanctuary where we can be ourselves, unguarded and unobserved, and fall into each other's embraces for hours upon hours. My heaven, my haven, my home. How would our families react if they knew? They believe we sit here reading and sketching and exchanging pleasantries. Little Marian's head might explode with the discovery, though it may well do her some good; I do not imagine she's ever kissed anyone or even touched herself down there. I should, as the elder sister, speak with her about pleasure and share my knowledge. My, how that would awaken her from her stupor. Or it may be that she is saucier than I could ever imagine? No. Very unlikely.

For a few months now, we have had our kissing and pleasure in our private domain, tucked into the trees, protected against the colder weather and rain the season now brings, but the little thing torments me further every day.

After all these weeks and months together, I need to know how she feels about me and our future together. I cannot invest such time and energy into wooing her and planning our future if she may strike off with another at even the poorest of marriage proposals. I tell her we need to commit to each other, it is only fair. She refuses to give me an answer despite my insistence. I said she could have until my birthday next April, months away, and she promises it sooner, but still delays.

She is as bad as Marian and Father with her indecision. How have any of them survived this long? At least with Miss Walker the indecision can be explained, partly, by her mollycoddled upbringing where the poor thing didn't have to make a single decision for herself until her parents died. It is their fault for raising such a meek child, so dependent on others. The only chance she stood was being watched over by her brother, who by all accounts sounded delightful, but then he went and died on his honeymoon, selfishly leaving a widow with child, later stillborn, and his two hopeless sisters. What chance did they stand?

This waiting on an answer makes me anxious and I snap at her. It's been months. How hard can it be? I wish she would just choose. It is not a matter of life and death. It is a matter of love and surely, if she loves me she will commit to me and if she does not love me then she will not, and we can quit this ridiculous charade. Of course, I will miss our kisses. But the Moss House does not have her name over the door. I will find someone else to enjoy it with.

Damn her, why does she plague my mind even when she is not with me?

Miss Walker

How can I tell her? What will she think of me? We have kissed and more in her Moss House. Months have passed, and I have remained dumb. I should have been grieving; I have acted too quickly. Now she wants commitment as if we are to be engaged. How can I tell her my fiancé has died, and not long before we first kissed in summer? Oh God, I am awful. I thought I loved him. I thought I was grieving. And yet one look at Miss Lister and all I wanted to do was to kiss her.

I shall write her a letter perhaps. Oh, that's cowardly, but she makes me afraid. She judges me unfairly. She cannot understand. She tells me she has never loved before me, though I'm sure that cannot be true. But if it is, and I am the first, can she bear that I have loved another?

Oh, my poor Mr Fraser. A sweet, gentle man, who would have loved me and protected me and treated me kindly.

How do I break this to Miss Lister?

Miss Lister

With my face under her skirts she tells me in a quick sentence that she was engaged to be married, but he died just before we met. I am dumbfounded. No hint of this revelation prior to this moment. I am lost for words. She looks at me and I cannot tell if she wants me to sympathise, be angry or just plain continue.

Somehow the latter does not feel appropriate, so I do the gentlemanly thing and lay her skirts back down and sit beside her, taking her delicate hand in mine. I do not speak, for fear of saying the wrong thing. I wonder if she loved him and think perhaps that's why she's been such a prig all this time. Is she grieving, and all this was an escape to take her mind off him? Oh, damn it, has she been using me?

Miss Walker

She holds my hand and looks at me earnestly. She does not speak so I feel I must go on. I'm very conscious of how hot I am suddenly and that it probably wasn't the perfect moment to broach this, but it's done. So, I explain.

Miss Lister

She starts to cry and reveals that she had been engaged to a man. He'd only been dead a month before she first kissed me and within four months, here she is sat on my knee and I with the taste of her on my lips.

She seems to have genuinely cared for the poor fellow and been prepared for marriage. Then a shock. Then I swagger in and assume she's single and available and just a bit of a prude. Does this change things between us? I'd rather hoped she had never had feelings for a man; that way I could be sure she felt as I do about women. To hear her declare that she was willing to marry a man makes me wonder about everything.

I manage to talk her from her tears with a thousand apologies. If I'd have known I would never have made any moves towards kissing her. We would have remained friends until she was past her grief. I would never have pressured her for a decision on our relationship if I'd have known she'd not long ago been engaged to another.

No wonder she could not give me a decision. But why keep a thing like that to herself? Does everyone know but me? What a fool. No wonder her aunt warned her off me if she thought I had no care for her grief.

I listen to her talk about him; he sounds a fool, but nice enough, and handsome she tells me, as if I care. Penniless of course. If he'd been a Count, I could have seen his love as genuine, but the Walker sisters are a good catch for their wealth. Surely she saw this. She's better off with him dead.

After hearing of her grief, I think back over the last months at how it explains her hesitance but does not explain her passionate kisses at all. She cannot have liked him *that* much. I wonder how far she got with him? Did he touch her and hold her as I have? Was he larger than me, stronger, were his kisses rough, did his stubble scratch her delicate face?

Miss Walker

How can I feel so torn? I love her, in truth. I love every moment with her. The newfound sanctuary of our little place in the woods. I feel safe in her presence, her touch, I lose myself in her arms, but the moment I think of our future together, think that what we are doing may be wrong, a storm grows inside me that I cannot control. I feel guilty, a sinner, as though all this will be snatched away from me, that it is all just a dream to be woken from.

Miss Lister

Just days later in the Moss House again she seems quite recovered from her confession and laughs and jokes about other things. I take the opportunity to pick her up and place her on the floor before the fire. I lean over her and have my hand up her skirts before she can protest. I wonder if he had her? She does not resist, and I give her pleasure, roughly, holding her down with forceful kisses to her mouth and neck as she squirms. She sighs and hums with the joy of it. When she is done, I roll onto my back beside her and pleasure myself as she watches, caressing my hair and then my breasts through my blouse. She does not reach for my skin or go near my queer. It's still rather one-sided.

Miss Walker

I have told her how much I like her. I talk of our futures as if they are written together. We discuss Shibden as if it is the home of us both. I'd be happy to share my money with her for our joint endeavours. I am relieved to have found someone who does not want me just for my money; she wants me for me. When I am with her, in the moment, I forget the world outside, forget that we are the same, forget that we are not husband and wife, that what we are doing is wrong.

How can I shape this in my mind to understand it and be at one with it? Do I need to just be her companion and set aside all our intimacy? She tells me she would not speak to me if I were to marry another. She could not tolerate it. I suppose I could not either.

Miss Lister

A week later and it's a stormy day. We are in the Moss House with the fire blazing and the wind outside blowing through the trees and rattling the panes, and I find myself wondering if I love her. I can only compare her to Mariana and how she made me feel. Should I accept that this will be a different sort of love? With Mariana we were equals, though of course I was the husband. Equals in intellect, interests, desires, loves. We could talk about anything, freely.

With Miss Walker I feel superior. It is not her fault, but the relationship is different, like that of a teacher and her pupil, not just about intimate relations but in all things. She asks my advice as if she has no clue herself. It is not a discussion; she just accepts what I say. I could tell her all sorts of mistruths and she would believe me.

Can I think myself into being in love with her? She is not as pretty as Mariana, but she is pretty enough. Prettier than me. Is she my only option now?

It will serve Mariana right once she hears that I have moved on and she has no chance any longer. I may be happier with Miss Walker than previous women. Being the husband in this relationship may be more rewarding, to see her blossom and grow in confidence. This way we will argue less, and I can make all the decisions. Is that really what I want? I may have to find my intellectual equal elsewhere or I may grow bored by her quickly.

A few weeks more and the dark nights have crept in. She now seems to think I will only like her until the novelty wears off. I convince her I have never felt like this about anyone else before. I can tell she does not quite believe me, and I wish I'd never tried to lie. The lamp goes out and we continue to kiss, and I feel for her breasts and then down to her queer. She does not resist, and I whisper to her that it would break my heart if she left me. It is a mistake. She sits up, pushing me away. She recounts to me that she is still undecided and she has not committed to me yet. I must give her time, she insists, and she flies from the Moss House and out into the dark as if I had struck her.

I do not go after her.

Miss Walker

If I see her, I must be in her arms, touch her. This is not how friends should be. We do as much as men and women do, and gain pleasure from it. Now she tells me her heart can be broken while all along I believed it would be mine that would break. I believed that she would leave me and I would be devastated. That I could accept. For her to say that I could break her heart means that the decision of our lives is down to me. She loves me; I have her heart in my hands and it is too much for me to decide, too much responsibility to have another's life under my control. I love her, yes, but I am well prepared to be heartbroken. If she will not break my heart, then this is it. We are in love. Mutually and forever. How has this happened? This, what can I call it, this affair, has become something more; a relationship that has a standing. The two of us are in love. How can this be? How shall it end? For happiness eludes me, and I will steal it from her too. She loves a cursed and unworthy being, who will drain her of her happiness. I cannot bring that upon her. I wish she did not love me. I wish she would leave me, let me wallow in my melancholy. I cannot cope with this feeling that I am loved, I who am unworthy. How unwisely she has chosen!

She fears rightly that I will break her heart. I flee from her as I had hoped she would flee from me. I run out into the night, away from the Moss House, away from Miss Lister. Go and travel, see the world, leave this region to me alone. Leave me here in my safe place and I shall erase my memory of you. Travel far and do not return until after my death. Do not mourn me. You deserve to be loved by someone who can give you everything.

Do not love me. Do not let me break your heart.

Chapter Seven

Winter, 1832: A cold winter's walk and the expectation of an answer

Miss Lister

I walk the estate grounds every day, despite the frequent rains and colder weather. I have watched the trees change from summer to autumn and now walk amongst their fallen leaves as true winter sets in. It is not the same as the streets of Paris, but it has its own charm. As a child I would walk here often, but now it is mine. Well, a third of it at least. One day, I hope it will all belong to me. To stand on ground that one owns is remarkable. I feel fortunate; so few have this feeling in their lives. I could lie down right here and no one could make me move or take it away from me. I do not of course; I would look half mad.

As I walk, I examine where I would expand the beck at the bottom of the hill into a lake and where I would build a driveway to a gatehouse adjoining the main road from Halifax. I imagine it already complete.

I've planted more trees, creating a woodland which will outlive me. I have plans for a waterfall and ponds. Wherever I walk, it always leads me to my beloved Moss House. Even alone I can spend hours there in peace, undisturbed.

The fresh air does me good. Being indoors for too long makes me anxious; walking frees my mind. I will venture out each day despite the weather, even just for an hour. I quite enjoy the rain on my face and the cold wind that creeps in at my cuffs and collar.

How could she not enjoy this? The glorious summers and bleak winters of Yorkshire – extremes of temperature to make you appreciate the other, and all that's in between. Grateful for a temperate day where you do not need gloves or to hold onto your hat. Grateful for a day of sunshine, so rare they are blessed.

How does she not wish to ascend to the high points? Up Beacon Hill where they hung the bodies of criminals, but such a beautiful spot overlooking the town and the hills, the routes in and out. You can see a storm cloud from over Hebden Bridge way as it heads towards you and race it back down to the Hall and have the fire lit before it hits. How can she not be in awe of our views, and enjoy looking out over what she owns? Nothing quite compares, although being atop a summit in the Pyrenees is close. A different vista altogether, beautiful, but not home, not my own. The question I received most often after I had achieved the ascent, some five years ago now, was not 'was it difficult?', but 'why?'. Why, they would ask, did I want to ascend a mountain? Why ever not? I thought. It was because I wanted to know what ten thousand feet high felt like, compared to the one thousand feet I climb here in my home region. I wanted to know if my body could carry me so high into the sky. I wanted to know if I would feel any different, being so much closer to God and the Heavens. I wanted to because no woman had done so before me. I will ascend another mountain again soon. This time I'd like to be the first person ever to climb it, male or female. Why, they ask me? Because I can.

I enter the Moss House and it feels empty without her. I may have mentioned moving into Shibden together a bit too soon. Telling her that she would break my heart if she left me must have been too much. I can be rather romantic sometimes. But to run off like a schoolgirl...!

Miss Walker

I walk to the farthest part of the gardens on the edge of the wood. The woods lure me in, but I stop. It is as if I am standing on the edge of civilization, the well-mown grass, planted flowers and gravel pathways a place of human-built structures, but if I were to take just one more step the world around me would change into the wilderness of unkempt grounds, of mud and leaf-fall and the trees rising up either side blocking out the light and stretching before me as far as I can see, as if, were I to enter them, I would be held inside the woods for eternity. I fear that if I walk too far into the woods, I shall turn around and it will have closed in behind me and I will never find my way out. So I stand on the precipice, where I can admire the trees but I cannot be lost in them. I gaze into the woods with no end for as long as I can before a chill rises in me and I turn quickly back to face the house, the safe place where it is warm, and I am surrounded by memories and portraits of ancestors with whom I have been familiar my whole life, though never having known them. I want to rush back, but I make myself stand on the edge for as long as I can bear it.

Loneliness is silent. Does she feel it too? The world so large, the skies above and the Earth beneath and we small beings perched on the top, held perfectly. Wherever we go we touch the Earth, unable to float up or sink down. It steadies me. The few times I have ventured farther than I have known before, I have felt there has not been enough air. The Earth seems to move differently; it is not the piece of ground I know. It is not Walker land where my ancestors stood. God can find me if I am here. How will He watch over me if I wander? Does He see me in the Moss House? Does He see me here on the edge of the woods, like a tethered horse who can only graze in a circle? Does the tether give the horse security, or does she long to run free?

With Miss Lister I can walk farther. Even though my feet become sore and my back aches, when holding her arm I feel as if I could walk around the world. I do not turn to look for home, as she becomes the point to which I am tethered and she holds me firm. She likes to walk up towards High Sunderland Hall from where she can look down on her estate. I am happy standing beside her, but if she were to leave me there, I would come undone.

When I was young, my father walked me up to Beacon Hill, overlooking the town, and he told me it was where they hung the bodies of criminals to warn others not to break the law. There had been a gang who made money by clipping the edges off gold coins to make new ones. Clever indeed; but they were caught. The coiners were hanged in York and their bodies brought back here to be displayed in chains, their arms pointing back to the scene of their execution as a warning to others.

Someone gave them up. That was all it took, my father said. One person to tell tales and others' lives are ruined. I replied that what they were doing was wrong, and should they not be punished? He told me that not everything is simply right and wrong. Sometimes a wrong is right. Sometimes a right is wrong.

But the worst thing, he said, was telling tales. I swore to him that I would never tell tales.

Everyone else, however, seems very happy to do just that. The rumours I have been told about Miss Lister could furnish a novel of a most unbelievable character. I have even had anonymous letters warning me to steer clear of her, as if she were the Devil himself! Miss Lister is most kind. I believe that people are afraid of what they do not know. How brave of her to defy society – and what a clever way to do it too. But why of all colours choose black? Of all the forms her defiance could take, why that? Perhaps a different hairstyle, following a French fashion, would be better. I hear some women have even worn trousers. But to wear black takes courage, when single women are required to wear pale, neutral colours, as if advertising our innocence. Miss Lister defies that. I believe that is why people are so concerned about my acquaintance with her. If she wears black, what else will she do? Little do they know! They are too naive and small-minded to ever know her true secret: that she can give me pleasure no man would ever manage. That she is a woman with a man's heart, a man's passion.

Would I prefer her to be more feminine? Wear colour? Or is it her difference, her defiance that makes her so... unique? I would never tell tales on her, even if my life depended on it. For she could tell tales on me too. Whom would they believe? Perhaps we would both be cast aside as deviants, criminals, witches, and hung in chains over Beacon Hill for all to see the warning that women of Halifax must do as they are told.

Miss Lister

I wonder if her reluctance to commit to me is because of my appearance. Is she ashamed of my looks? While we hide away in the Moss House in secret I am acceptable to her, but when she thinks of being aligned with Miss Lister as a sort of partnership – is that what makes her afraid? Is she so concerned about what others think? Can I do anything to address that? For her, would I change myself? Would I conform and wear colour? Pastels and pinks and ribbons and bows, all trussed up like a parcel to be admired and chosen and doted upon? In the face of it all I chose black. The gracefulness of it. And it does not show the dirt. Black is my colour until the day I die. For I am like no other – let them see it and judge what they will, for I shall not be deterred.

If she were to love me, she should love me for who I am. But if I love her, should I not be willing to change for her? This sounds as though it may be a ponderance of many couples over the centuries. She should take me as I am, for this is me. To wear colours, bonnets and ribbons, to leave the estate work to the men, to curb my travels and never ascend another mountain, is that what she asks of me? Then it is not me she loves.

I send her a note as I will not let this end from my own lack of trying. Let her explain herself to me if she wants to break this off. She replies I may visit and invites me to see her. She does not mention the Moss House. I wonder if this is the end. I march to Crow Nest, thinking all the while I am to be cast aside, probably with paltry excuses. I am angry. Can she not see that I care? I am happy to give her my time, my energies, my love.

I shall stand in silence to hear what she has to say first. If it is disagreeable to me, I shall bid her farewell.

As I walk up over the valley and towards the Walker lands, I wonder if this may be the last time I ever come this way. If I walk back broken-hearted, I shall never wish to see an inch of Walker estate again. I shall leave here and all the hopes that have risen in me that this could be my home and that I had found someone to share it with at last. All dashed because she is too timid to see what happiness is offered to her.

I decide to call in on her aunt first. Make her wait. I must keep up appearances that I am friends with all the Walker family, not just one of them.

I am blunt with her aunt and ask her what vexes her niece. I ask if she has ever left home before, what she can tell me of her fiancé? It is wicked of me, but if Miss Walker will not tell me herself, I shall find out. Her aunt does not give much away at first, though I construct my questions as those from a most innocent and concerned friend. What she reveals makes it sound as though she should warn *me* away from her niece rather than the other way around. I tell her that I did not know about her fiancé until just recently so was unaware of her grief when we first met. I gush that I would never have pursued her for such happy walks and company had I known she was so grieved. Her aunt seems to let me into her confidence and tells me of her little niece's bouts of melancholia and a bad back which pains her all the time. I tell her, honestly, that she seems much more confident since our acquaintance and has joined me on walks, a little farther each time and, before long, the old judgemental gossip cannot but agree that I have been of benefit to her niece.

As I approach Crow Nest, I wish for a moment that I lived in one of the grand Walker properties. Such a funny name, Crow Nest, like a pirate ship; but I can see why she likes it, with its high ceilings and opulence, marble instead of wood, high carved fireplaces and servants for your every need. It makes Shibden seem less grand, despite its ancestry. This new house is angled correctly, everything so square. I am lured by its architecture into feeling more highborn than I am. Would I wish to be the owner of this house, instead of Shibden? But Shibden is hundreds of years old, its beams have seen generations!

For all my worrying, as soon as we are behind closed doors Miss Walker lays in my arms on the sofa, her bad back obviously taking a day off from the constant pain her aunt reported. I kiss her, but not as passionately as I would like. Am I falling out of love already? She begs forgiveness for running out on me and begs for more time to make her decision, as usual. As if to prove that I should wait, she takes me up to her bedroom and we kiss and press ourselves together, but that is all. I daren't do much. I let her steer us and she seems content with our closeness. Should I never ask for more? As we lie here, I know this is not enough for me. I've had this before; women who want to kiss, want you to flatter them and hold them and caress them, but you never reach their skin. They do not realise it is a tease, a torture even. While they are satisfied and flattered and excited, it is not enough for me. It is a half-truth.

Despite the many pleasures she has received from me, she is never entirely naked. She has always resisted me fully taking off her clothes, so I must grapple to reach her beneath them. Now, as she lies before me, she may as well be in a suit of armour. We have taken a step backwards. A step back to being friends who play with kisses, like girls practising for someone else.

I leave Crow Nest and all its modern opulence feeling disheartened and stomp all the hour's walk back to Shibden. I busy myself in the study and draw up some plans for landscaping around the Hall and a new approach road.

I suffer through supper with my family of bores and retire early to be miserable alone. I even guessed the temperature wrong this morning. I should have known it would be a bad day.

Miss Walker

It was two days after I fled the Moss House that she came to see me. She sent me a note to ask permission to visit and I replied straight away with a yes. Two long, torturous days. She forgave me and waited for me to explain, but how could I without weeping and sounding half mad? She could not understand my anguish. I wanted to prove to her I loved her too and so sat by her on the sofa and we kissed and as the words did not flow, I took her to my room and held her.

She was changed. Colder. My own fault entirely. I shall have to find a way to explain to her my mind. Then she will be more patient with me, more forgiving, and not read my fleeing as from *her*, but as from *myself.*

I shall wear more black. Show my allegiance to her. However, I do not own a single black garment, except my mourning clothes. I shall purchase a new shawl. A beautiful black lace shawl. I wonder if she will notice?

Would I wish to live at Shibden as she suggests? It is cosy. I like the company she has of her aunt, father and sister and they seem to like me well enough. It is busier there than here and feels more alive. I may quite like to live somewhere like Shibden Hall with its wooden panelled walls and large fires, so tucked away from the world.

But here there are happy memories of when we were small. I remember how we would play in the entrance hall on the black and white tiles like a chessboard. The black tiles, should you stand on them, would fall away and drop you into Hell. The white tiles were safe and solid like the Earth. Although fanciful, the fear grew innate and even now, I step delicately along the white tiles. Just a few weeks ago I dropped a glove and as it fell towards a black tile, I honestly believed for a moment that it would disappear as if down a hole.

Moving away from here may be best for me after all. I should consider it.

How do I explain to her my silly exit from the Moss House? I'd felt a panic rising and didn't want her to see. I dashed out into the trees to catch my breath and let my tears out. I hoped she would come for me, but the door stayed closed. I waited, but the woods closed in and I had to summon all my courage to march back up to the Hall. Luckily I saw her groom and asked him to take me home. What must he think of us? He readied the horses quickly, but there was enough time... and she did not come for me.

I had a dream that I was on a life-sized chess set, full of pieces. I was a pawn on the front row, waiting to be moved forward in sacrifice. Miss Lister was behind me, the king. She gave the orders for pieces to move and watched them fall as she made notes for her diary. She moved me onto a black square and as I fell, I heard her laugh. A triumphant laugh, as if she had won. Miss Lister will always win.

Chapter Eight

Winter, 1832: An awkward interruption and a Happy New Year

Miss Lister

Christmas is upon us. A new year dawns. I carry on with business as usual for Shibden. I can barely keep on top of the estate, yet even so my precious time is ever more taken up with wooing Miss Walker.

I am now begging for her affections. I hear myself tell her she need only love me a quarter as much as I love her, and I'd be happy. What foolish words! When did I become so meek? I hear myself mewling and dislike what she has made me, yet I am still optimistic she will submit. I know I must be gentle but am reminded by my reflection that I may not have many more chances to find love. How long do I wait for her returned affection, when she, twelve years my junior, could easily try again with man or woman?

I am changed. I told my aunt, in whom I'd previously confided about my desire for us to set up home together, that it will not work. I gave the excuse that Miss Walker will not give up Crow Nest, nor I Shibden. I will give up Miss Walker instead. I look back over my diary pages and see the times she has cried, changed her mind, left me frustrated. She should be lucky to have me. Finally, several months from our first kiss, I decide I shall move on without her. I feel somewhat relieved.

Mrs Priestley visits with her usual festive cheer and a hamper of delights for our family. She tells me she thinks my visiting Miss Walker this year has been good for her and she's noticed a considerable change in her demeanour since meeting me and spending time with me. That will be all the orgasms, I want to tell her, but keep that to myself.

I may be good for her, but I doubt now that Miss Walker has been any good for me.

With nothing else to amuse me I venture to her house again to give my own Christmas greetings. I am all set to end it, but it seems cruel at this time of year so I secretly hope the season of goodwill will prompt her to make up her mind. I will give her until the end of January.

As I stomp over to her estate in the bitter cold, leaving my family around a warm fire with wine, I remember how each time I head over this way I believe it may be the last. How long can we keep this game up? I start to think again of travel plans for next year. I have my atlas out at the ready. Nothing prevents me leaving but her. Let us see how far she is prepared to go for me. One last try.

After a few glasses of wine, I get my hand up her skirts and she allows me, but keeps her thighs pressed together so all I feel is her drawers. She asks me if I will stay with her and keep her warm for the night. The way she says it is not in the least arousing; I'm aware she means fully clothed. It is torturous to be so close to her, but the barriers of cloth and frigidity are as insurmountable as a ten-foot wall.

I refuse to stay and angrily stomp all the way back again to Shibden, close myself in my room and take my own pleasure, several times. I am too annoyed to sleep so get back up and read some of my diary, once again looking back over the months since I met her. If I was looking on at my own situation, I would firmly advise myself to give up on her.

Miss Walker

I receive word from my dear friend Mrs Ainsworth that she would like to visit in the new year. We have known each other since we were children. We were so close until she married. I have not seen her now for many years, but we always write at Christmases and birthdays. Unfortunately, she says she will be coming with her husband. How I wish she would come alone, but at least I will see her. I can talk to her freely, not about everything, of course, but I can tell her of my friendship with Miss Lister and what she proposes; that we shall live together as companions and have a joint household and swear to never marry. Mrs Ainsworth may think us peculiar, but she will hopefully see that it makes sense. I'll not mention the Moss House. I'll not look her husband in the eye. I'll not be afraid of him.

Miss Lister has it in her head for us to take a trip to York in the new year. She wants me to see a doctor about my aching back and to see if he can advise me on why I am so tired, when Miss Lister, twelve years older than me is able to wake up with a strength and vigour I've never possessed and walk farther than I could dream of. Miss Lister acts as if seeing him is urgent, but I know I have always been this way and other doctors have never found a cure for my back. I think the real reason to go is that she wants to visit old friends and introduce me.

When I mentioned Miss Lister's suggestion of a visit to Doctor Belcome to Mrs Priestley, she tells me he is brother to Mrs Lawton; Miss Lister's friend Mariana. The way she said her name made me think Miss Lister was very close to her. Mrs Priestley is innocent of Miss Lister's real desires, so would think nothing of it – but I feel a pang of jealousy. Who was Mrs Lawton to her?

I attend the usual family gatherings over Christmas but whilst there think about the Listers and wish I was with them at Shibden. I bravely smile and dance and have enough wine to keep my spirits up and face my family, all gossiping about my new friend, asking when am I to be wed and what the Listers are like? Elizabeth and the children come down from Scotland, which brings such relief and company for me, but *he* is with them too. He gets drunk and offends Mr Priestley and looks at me with leering eyes. I hide in the drawing room with Elizabeth and the children until his dominating presence appears and claims her, and I am left with warm wine and sleeping children in my arms. The rest of the house is filled with laughter and merriment and all I want is to be with Miss Lister. Thankfully she says she will come over on New Year's Eve and keep me company once this annual family pother is over with.

Miss Lister

On New Year's Eve, despite the cold outside and the cold creeping around my heart, I find myself wishing my family a happy New Year early and take the carriage over to Crow Nest as I promised her I would. I'm not sure why I am bothering. My beloved Moss House has been a single-person dwelling these last few weeks.

However, not long after my arrival when we are ensconced in her living room, her servants forget their role to knock on the door and announce guests, and so our dear friend, Mrs Priestley, who has come to offer good tidings for the New Year, swans straight in and catches us in each other's arms.

I jump up by the fire, but Miss Walker is red. None of us know what to say and I am not sure how long she has been stood there, watching. After a few moments of silence, Mrs Priestley turns and leaves.

We must be aroused by this discovery as instead of running after our dear friend and trying to explain, we begin kissing again and then race to her bedroom. This time she allows me to remove her clothes, all except her stockings as she is chilly, and under the bedclothes our skin presses against each other's and my hands freely touch all the hair and skin of her queer with no clothing in the way. I run my hands all over her body, which finally is mine to caress and squeeze as I feel down each of her legs and the softness of her buttocks and run my hands behind her, arching her up towards me as I run my tongue down her neck, between her breasts, kissing her belly and protruding hip bones, then down into her hair. I move so I can kiss her, truly kiss her down there, and find her opening with my tongue and gently push it inside and around her; licking, kissing, sucking, my hands holding hers by her sides as she groans with pleasure. She mumbles for me to stop but I push harder with my tongue, harder and faster, her hands clasped in mine, her legs writhing on the bed and her breath coming faster and faster.

Thank you, Mrs Priestley!

I rather hoped she would walk in a second time. This would confirm without a shadow of a doubt my intentions towards innocent Miss Walker – but this time the door was firmly locked.

Miss Walker cannot help but let out a cry as her body shudders. I release her hands and sit back, pulling off all the covers to see her fully naked for the first time, hot and flushed. For a moment she lies there, allowing the pleasure to subside, her eyes closed, her delicate lower lip clenched between her perfect teeth, arms outstretched, legs apart, beautiful, vulnerable, mine.

Then of course, she remembers all her insecurities and pulls the covers back over herself. I slump beside her and begin to kiss her again. I tell her how beautiful she looks, and she softens, allowing me to move in close to her and pull her body against mine, skin against skin. I hold her closely. How can I make her confident? How can I make her free? Seemingly encouraged, she reaches down and remembering how I pleasure her with my fingers she does the same to me. She is no expert and so takes some time, but the excitement of seeing her whole body for the first time allows me to succumb and then we fall asleep in each other's arms.

I dream that a dragon comes to take over Shibden and he will not leave unless I sacrifice Miss Walker to him, and in the dream, I do. I do not hesitate. I wake up feeling guilty, but she has already risen and redressed as if nothing has happened.

Miss Walker

Oh dear, there is nothing I can do. I am no good at lying. If Mrs Priestley were to ask me out loud, or even in a letter, I would have to tell her the truth. It's been a week now since New Year and no word from her since she ran from Crow Nest. I should have gone after her, perhaps told her I'd been upset over something and that Miss Lister was comforting me – but I do not know how much she saw. Miss Lister said that she must have seen enough to be certain for her to have left like that. She will probably never speak to either of us again. I've lost a friend! What if she tells others about us? Mr Priestley, my cousins, my aunt?

Then to have done what I did afterwards! Instead of going after her, begging forgiveness, telling her I'd been led astray, that I would never see Miss Lister again, instead I take her up to my bedroom and allow her to... like a common whore! Oh, how low I have fallen!

But can I really blame Miss Lister when I have been complicit all along? This is what I want, this pleasure. These desires come from me. Everyone will now know anyway – why do I not just move in with her and hide away at Shibden? I will not have to face anyone else again. I am an independent woman of means with no need for any contact with my family and friends. If they do not like what I am then so be it! They are no friends of mine. It seems because I am different from all that's expected of me that Miss Lister is my only true equal. I shall be with her alone. She will be enough for me.

My mind is made up. My answer is yes. I will be her companion, partner, whatever she wishes. I will commit to her.

I'll ask Mrs Ainsworth what she thinks when she arrives. I value her opinion. She has never met Miss Lister and does not know the politics of our families and estates. I will not, of course, tell her everything, but she can help me decide. I wish she would visit alone! Her husband is best avoided; he reminds me too much of an indiscretion, something I have tried hard to forget. I write to her and say I am unwell and wish for her to visit me alone as it will be tiresome for her husband with no male company.

Miss Lister

January races on and we meet regularly at the Moss House. We are both naked more often now, and giving and receiving pleasure as if we are a married couple. Will she commit to me? She still will not tell me what her mind is. She tells me she is too worried about Mrs Priestley. She changes the subject to her friend Mrs Ainsworth who will be coming to visit shortly and how we shall show her the sights of Halifax. I tell her it will be a quick trip, but she does not laugh. She promises a decision by the end of January, assuming my offer is still on the table. I do nothing to correct her.

This Ainsworths' visit in January that she talks of may do her good. Mrs Ainsworth seems to be a close friend and Miss Walker tells me she'll ask her advice about my offer. They have known each other since they were children. I suggest she could rent one of her properties to them – she would have an income from it and gain friends nearby. She likes the idea at first, but it appears she is more friends with the wife than the husband, and she then seems to change her mind and conclude that a visit will suffice. I hope Mrs Ainsworth may help Miss Walker decide to move in with me.

I have booked for us to visit Doctor Belcome in York soon and we shall see what he can advise about her back. She moans all the time about it and yet seems quite happy to just sit and not lift a thing to exercise it. I rub it for her gently and it feels as good a back as any other I have felt. She seems so fragile; I hope Doctor Belcome can help me fix her, make her strong.

Miss Walker

My nerves remain on edge over Mrs Priestley, what gossip may spread, the Ainsworths visiting, giving Miss Lister a decision and now having to see a doctor. What on Earth shall I tell him? I surely cannot be honest with him... or perhaps he knows. Perhaps that's why Miss Lister wants to make such a trip to see him. Perhaps he is the only one in the world to whom I can talk freely. Perhaps he can give me some medicine to cure me of it. Cure me of these feelings. Quieten my mind.

I remember a piece of talk from many years back. A rumour about Miss Lister from when she was young. That her school friend went mad and was taken to the asylum in York. I'm sure that this is yet another reason why people wrote to warn me about her. No one could ever imagine her true secret or intentions towards me; they were not worried for my soul but for my mind. It seems that everyone in Halifax, in Yorkshire, in fact, knows that Miss Lister turned her school friend insane!

The girl is still locked in the asylum. Perhaps that's where Miss Lister is taking me. She's had enough of me and is going to have me declared insane by a doctor and locked away!

Chapter Nine

Winter, 1833: A carriage ride to York and news of an accident

Miss Lister

As the horses' hooves finally clatter onto the cobblestones of York, I feel at home. An excitement rises in me as we travel through the gatehouse in the high city walls, through the bustling streets as the carriage heads up towards the Minster. I insist on taking Miss Walker there first. Though she protests tiredness, she has never seen it before and so I drag her there in confidence she will be in awe of it as I have been every time I have visited.

It is a cold January morning but the sun shines brightly, as though God Himself is reminding us of His presence. I sit her down in a central pew and tell her of its history, the architecture, the import of those buried here and the stories captured in the beautiful glass. I show her the damage by the fire just a few years before and the work undertaken to restore its former glory. She sits in wonderment and I slide my arm around her – I cannot help myself. I feel privileged to share this with her, see the delight of a new discovery on her face. I cannot wait to take her to new lands, new cities, new cultures, beyond anything she can imagine from her life in Yorkshire. The heat abroad will do her good too. I vow that this will be her last winter in these cold climes. I shall take it upon myself to find us a place in southern France where we can retire for warmer winters. I shall make her strong again.

As she sits in the pew, following my finger with her gaze as I point at some marvel or other, I see that she is beautiful, as if coming into full bloom so many years after she should have done, but she is managing it at last. I am the gardener who has tended her roots, fed and watered her, sheltered her and now am planting her into the world itself.

Of course, she starts to fidget and says she is still cold from the carriage, that the cobbles have made her back ache and she cannot concentrate on much, knowing she is to see a doctor tomorrow. Can we get that over with first, she says, and then she will enjoy herself more, treat me to some gifts in the shops and buy us tea. I, however, could sit here for hours, and if she had been any other companion I may have sent her back to the carriage and on to the hotel without me while I wandered the streets or walked the walls, but I do not wish to leave her, or her to leave me. York is not going anywhere so I escort her dutifully back to the carriage and once at the hotel I order tea to be brought to our rooms and send out my groom to buy some sweet pastries and, if he can find it, a book about the Minster which I can read to her. Soon the fire is lit and we sit together on the sofa before it. I cover her with every blanket I can find and slide myself in next to her, giving her all my heat as she sips gracefully at her tea. The pastries arrive and we eat them most unladylike without plates or napkins and let the crumbs fall where we sit. I lick her fingers clean.

Whilst she fears our visit tomorrow, I look forward to it. I hope to learn what I can do for this delicate bird. Then I hope she will be calmer and start to see this as a short holiday. The first of many, I hope. I privately hope Doctor Belcome will tell us that travel will do her good and agree with my prescription of warmer weather to aid her back and her constant chills. After the visit, I will introduce her to my York friends, the Best sisters, both excellent painters, and their mother, and take her over to Langton Hall to my long-serving friend Isabella and her siblings, always such fun to be around – at least until the tragedy of my last visit. I have tried to put that behind me. They do not suspect a thing, but I am concerned that the longer I leave another visit, the more suspicion may arise. I must be sure not to start to fret at the memory of all the blood... I put it from my mind.

I would write to my friends straight away and arrange visits, but I am afraid that if tomorrow does not go well, I may have to return little Miss Walker post-haste back to Crow Nest. If so, I shall have to come back again without her, though it will not be the same. I want her with me as I walk the walls, visit the tower on the knoll, take a boat down the river. The thought of doing those things alone, as I so often have, now seems lonely to me. She has lured me into such a sense of companionship that, if it were to end, my days may never be the same.

Miss Walker

One moment I forget, the next moment I remember. One moment I feel free, the next moment I feel dread. One moment I am with her and she is my world, the next moment she is forcing me to do something I do not wish. One moment I feel as if I do not need a doctor, the next I feel as if only a doctor can save me.

I stare into the fire and try to quieten my mind. It is delightful here; these rooms, her arms around me, the sweet taste in my mouth; I finally feel warm. But tomorrow looms over me as if a shadow stands just behind me and reminds me of its presence with a chill that runs down my neck each time I momentarily forget.

I managed the coach ride in her company and quite enjoyed the view with my private tour guide who knows every building, hill and sheep on the way. I enjoy her talk when she gets into her tutor role; I can just listen. She does not expect a response and so I lose myself to the motion of the carriage and the sound of her voice and the passing views behind the glass pane.

I knew I would love the Minster and had I not been so cold from the journey I could have sat there for hours. I should like to return another day when I do not have something pressing on my mind, when it is summer perhaps, and my back does not torment me – but only ever with her by my side. I should not wish to be here with anyone but her. If she should disappear, I fear I will never leave Crow Nest again.

She reassures me Doctor Belcome is most kind and patient, and will not commit me to an asylum. She swears that as long as she lives, she will never let anyone take me away from her. She reassures me with some remarkable studies I'd rather not hear, of the types of women who are locked up, of true madness and its manifestations. She says the most I have is melancholy and a bad back, and that both are curable.

I tell her I have read there is cholera in York and I know I have just the ill luck to catch it, but she tells me that we will keep ourselves to the clean streets and away from any sickness.

Doctors before have told me they could cure me. Not just for the pains in my back, but for pains inside my head and heart which Miss Lister knows nothing of.

I'd been a happy girl with such potential. I used to be brave, but at seventeen I made a decision to visit my childhood friend who had just married a Mr Ainsworth in Derbyshire. In that one choice, that one trip, which should have been delightful, my world crashed down around me.

My family tried so many ways to move me past the turmoil which drew from me all my strength and tears and took me into silence for a very long time. I lost myself as they tried different medicines and methods. They took me up to Harrogate to bathe in cold waters. I was given tonics, talked at, kept warm, kept cold, given lots of certain foods and denied others, kept in my room, made to sit outside, watched at all times, doors locked; and through all of it, it was as if I was not there. No one talked to me as others answered on my behalf. I became ensconced inside a shell of myself, just waiting for the day when I would have the strength to crawl back out again.

Despite all the trials and different doctors, it was not a cure that saved me; I just came back into myself. One day, with no more tears to fall, I woke. I rose and washed and dressed and ate breakfast and carried on. For what can any of us do in truth but carry on? Over the next few months my strength returned. I walked to the edge of the woods and back. I began eating and writing letters again. I ordered some new novels to read and lost myself in their stories. With each one I became more awake, more myself.

Then, just a few years later, it all happened again when my parents died. I managed to get through it eventually with help from my siblings but then both of them married and left me.

97

It was as if my recovery allowed them to move on. They had both been dutiful and patient, so I was happy for them to have found love. But we would never see John again, his widow left carrying his child. I wonder where she is now? The Walkers cared little for her after the stillborn child. Elizabeth is gone too, so far away from me. I always knew she would leave me one day; I just wish she were happier.

Miss Lister

Doctor Belcome says there is nothing wrong with Miss Walker and that if she had to work for a living, she'd be fine. He writes down her maladies as nervousness and weak muscles. He agrees that travel will do her good and tells me not to pet her too much. He speaks to me as if I am her husband. I rather like it. I just wish I had a less nervous and weak-muscled wife to present to him. I wonder if Mariana ever confided in him about us? I wonder what a doctor would make of it? Would he suggest a cure? Or as a scientist, make no judgement? He is a married man with children, an educated man, who sees all people at their most vulnerable. But even so, I decide that our secrets will remain secret.

Miss Walker and I agreed beforehand that she could speak about anything except for our intimacy. For that alone would no doubt be deemed the reason for her melancholy, despite taking place long after her worst bouts of 'turmoil' as she calls it. Any doctor, even a kind one like Doctor Belcome may latch onto any deviation, any sin as he may see it, as the cause for all woes, regardless of the chronology. Men's sexual deviation is a problem of the mind, they say, that should be stopped and punished. What would they think of our deviation? I have it settled in my own mind that what we do as two single women

98

cannot possibly be in the same realm as happenings between two men, which is expressly forbidden by law. With Mariana it became complicated when she married, for then what we did was wrong: we were having an affair and committing adultery. I was with a married woman, and even though we had had a marriage ceremony of our own, her marriage to Lawton was legally binding and in the eyes of God. Each time I would see her I had to pray for forgiveness. Miss Walker and I are two single ladies seeking pleasure. Mildly sinful perhaps, but not illegal and not adultery.

I wonder if Doctor Belcome knows his sister's secrets? What would his advice have been? I shall ask her when I next see her if she ever spoke to her brother in openness. I would love to have a confidant like that. For years I was lucky to have Mariana; we shared everything while we were together. However, over the years, despite our travels together, our openness decreased, and I couldn't very well discuss other lovers with her. I skirt around it with my aunt, who I believe has her suspicions, and as lovely as she is would never ask outright. My father must know, but treats me as a novelty and never comments. Marian, I believe, has no clue at all.

As we leave Doctor Belcome's and head back to the hotel, Miss Walker seems more relaxed and talks of what we shall do over the next few days. No rushing back home to Crow Nest, then!

I know I must be delicate and I gently discuss his advice with her; some travel, a warmer climate, companionship. I suggest perhaps she may consider moving into Shibden again, so that we can be together all the time. She surprises me by agreeing. I wonder if Doctor Belcome suggested something similar and so now she will give it good consideration. Heaven forbid *I* should have advised it for several months now!

During our walks and shopping we choose a new dinner service we could buy between us. Something finer than either of us would choose alone, for if we pay half the costs each, we can buy the finest on offer. We decide not to buy it immediately, but she likes this idea of buying together nonetheless and goes so far as to suggest we go half each on a new bed for Shibden. I agree, more because she seems keen than for want of a new bed. It seems Doctor Belcome suggested a new bed to help her back. Whatever makes her happy, I shall agree to.

I rather like the idea of a joint household, and the thought of never worrying about finances again makes me feel excited for the future. When travelling, I am happy with an inn and a clean bed without lice, but Miss Walker's standards are higher, and I could grow accustomed to that as much as I have grown accustomed to her.

We talk of what she will busy herself with once we return to Halifax, as if going home after these few days will be a new start for her, as if being told she is not insane has released her from any obligation to act so. I encourage her to take up French again in preparation for a trip to France in summer and she agrees, and so seems set on my proposal to travel.

We buy each other gifts. I select her some music to play, something simple but beautiful and she promises she will learn it. Later that evening she tells me she will work towards a recital and invite some guests and that she will wear no drawers under her dress, just for me! York seems to have lifted Miss Walker nearer to my estimation of her. I wonder if it is her proximity to Crow Nest that drains her? Although I should not hark on about moving into Shibden for fear of pressuring her, I think it will be the best thing for both of us.

We call into several of the churches in York and she chooses a small one, Holy Trinity, as her favourite; tucked behind houses through a narrow brick path. Much like our Moss House, it is hidden from sight.

We see the travelling menagerie and she is amazed at the elephants, monkeys and a lion, the likes of which she has never seen before in her life. I watch the lion prowl before us, then sit obediently before the tamer as he commands him with his whip. I admire the bravery of the tamer, to face this majestic creature that stares at him through intelligent eyes and for some reason obeys him, whilst both lion and tamer know that at any moment, without motivation or fear of the consequence, the lion could decide to kill him and could do it in an instant. The tamer's power over the lion is an illusion they both agree to, but who really decides? The lion chooses an easier life, to obey and be fed and not whipped, of course he does, but at what point will he change his mind? What would it take for him to decide it is not worth it? Does he remember his youth, the freedom he was taken from, the desire to hunt, procreate, kill? As I watch, I will him to have a memory, to forget the bars and cages, the whips and commands, and show us what made him the king of the animals. Miss Walker trembles as she watches, and I long for him to bite the tamer's head off. Remind us that none of us can be contained, controlled, bullied without trying to break free. The lion tamer survives; the lion returns to his cage and is fed. I am somewhat disappointed.

After four joyous days we drive back home, watching out of the window as the gently rolling hills slowly grow in height until the familiar views loom up before us and the landscape turns dramatic. She comes with me to Shibden with no inclination to rush to her own home, which surprises me, and we settle in with the family, who are very accepting of Miss Walker's presence. She retires early and my family rush to tell me how much better Miss Walker looks after her trip and ask what Doctor Belcome said. I wonder if they are nosy or genuinely care for her. Probably both. I see how easy it would be for her to slip into life here at Shibden.

The next morning she tells me she needs to go home urgently, and without much explanation she packs in haste and says she will go with or without me. I had thought her previous actions revealed her decision at last to commit to me and even reside at Shibden, but when I ask her, she turns to me much changed from these last few days and says she must go home and ask Mrs Ainsworth's opinion. I ask her bluntly if the doctor also advised her never to make a decision by herself, and she marches off without a goodbye. I let her call for the carriage herself and watch her leave from a window overlooking the courtyard where she cannot see me.

She has managed to hold up a mask for a while but has now let it slip. She is not changed at all! Will she ever leave all her pother behind? I believe she will carry it with her wherever she goes.

Miss Walker

I return home vexed. I feel so content in her company and at Shibden, her family seem accepting of me, it is safe there. But who am I to deserve it? I have not told her the whole truth about me. I did not tell it to the doctor either. He believes I have suffered grief. The grief for my parents, my brother, Mr Fraser, and that grief alone is the cause of my anguish. How can I ever share my real secret, not just about how I feel about Miss Lister, but about myself?

Soon, I must face him. The man who did this to me.

I sit down for some breakfast at Crow Nest and when the maid brings it, she has some letters for me. She tells me one was hand delivered as urgent this morning.

It stares up at me with my name and address written in angry, unrecognisable handwriting. I try to eat and ignore it, but my appetite has left me. Urgent, she said. I shake as I open it, all the possibilities of its content racing through my mind.

Mrs Ainsworth has been killed.

My dear friend has been killed.

She was thrown from an open carriage.

I wonder what she was doing, where she was going, whom was she with. Was she out to prepare for her visit to me? Is it my fault she made that journey? Why couldn't he have died and not her?

Is this what I must suffer in exchange for just four days of happiness? For momentarily feeling alive and with hope for a future of contentment and dare I say it, love – this is what I must pay as a price?

It happened just yesterday. Was it at the same time as we travelled back in the carriage from York? Was she travelling too, looking out at the changing countryside and then, what horror! To be killed. How would she have suffered? There are few details in the letter, so I torment myself with visions of her being hurled and trodden under the horses' feet and dying slowly in agony with no one to help her. Or thrown and landing on her head and the life being struck from her instantly, her skirts all asunder and her bonnet muddied. Or a simple fall, and she stood back up and brushed herself down but then later collapsed as something inside her had been broken, much like Mr Fraser. Damn Miss Lister for sharing with me her anatomy lessons!

What did she think of as she fell, as she lay dying? Was she afraid? Did she cry out, scream, see ghosts of those gone before, see God Himself reach down for her, or angels to escort her away?

I am ten years ago again. Standing at the side of my mother's bed as her eyes roll back and her body stills. She had suffered the loss of my father, then her own body's ailments. She had told me to be strong, carry on. Carry on to what?

I console myself that this time I have a friend. A friend who will hold me, comfort me, ask me how I feel, take me under her wing. I send her a poorly written note, asking her to come as soon as she can. I hope she will forgive me for leaving so quickly this morning. I should have stayed at Shibden, then I would never have seen the letter, or she may have been with me when I received it. She would be holding me right now. The tears fall, they will not stop, grief upon grief...

Then suddenly I realise it is from him and I throw down the letter in disgust. It is his signature, his writing, he has touched this! I run from the room, from the news, from the letter.

I am cursed.

Chapter Ten

Winter, 1833: A confession and a bout of melancholy

Miss Lister

Falling from a carriage. What an awful way to die. Quick, hopefully. But awful.

It seems Miss Walker may well be as cursed as she imagined. Perhaps I am safer without her in my life; I may live longer.

Lo and behold, all our plans are stopped in their tracks again. She is reverted to grief.

Who could have predicted this? I hold her, sit with her and try to be as patient as I can. I am not made for nursing and long for her to fall asleep so I can get some fresh air. I take the opportunity as she finally sleeps to stride away from Crow Nest and into the woods which close in around me. I enjoy the momentary solitude they create and lose myself wandering when I can no longer see anything but trees.

Before too long has passed, I dutifully return to the house to check on her. Her aunt arrives and I dally about, unsure of what to do as her aunt sits with her in her room. I busy myself in her home, writing letters and gently playing on her grand piano.

I wonder if all along I have been thinking of it the wrong way around. I could be the owner of Crow Nest, in all its newness. It's scarcely sixty years old, whilst Shibden is four hundred. There are advantages and disadvantages to both. Perhaps we could keep this house for our guests. Better still, I could decant my father and Marian here from Shibden. I imagine they'd love it. Then we could keep Shibden to ourselves, and my aunt of course. But do I really want to be part of the nouveau riche? The Listers are ancient landed gentry whereas the Walkers are new money. They have none of the lineage.

Her aunt stays for lunch and I must make small talk with her as Miss Walker will not leave her room to join us. Luckily, I can recount our York trip and I confide in her some of what Doctor Belcome said. She and I both sigh at the same time, knowing that all has been undone again with this tragic news. Finally, her aunt leaves and I spend the rest of the day with Miss Walker alone, barely speaking a word.

I have read that in grief one is best to be just company. One is required merely to sit. Be present. Allow the person to grieve. How long will it last, I wonder? If it is months or years as I hear it was when her parents died, and then her brother, there is no way I could manage it, no matter what my feelings are for her. I wonder if I am best to leave her – not now, that would be heartless, but in a few weeks. I could take a trip for a few months and return afresh when she has recovered.

I stay until evening and though she begs me not to leave, I cannot cope. I make excuses and retire, promising I will be back for breakfast and that I have no plans to leave her any time soon. I just hope a few weeks is not 'soon' in her mind.

I care for her, I want to support her, I tell myself over and over as I ride in the carriage back over to Shibden ready to update the family about what new woe has befallen our little adopted flower.

Miss Walker

I should have kept us as friends and rejected her advances and not joined her in the Moss House all those days, not walked with her, especially into Halifax where people would see us together. Is God Himself judging me? Just as I began to feel some happiness and strength return to me, I have been dashed down onto the rocks and am helpless again.

Miss Lister

Another long dull day at Crow Nest. As I take the hour's walk back to Shibden I see the Hall for what it is: run down, old, falling apart. It even sounds shabby. I shall rebuild it as a castle and it will be Shibden Castle. Or better still, Lister Castle. Yes, that's where I shall live.

Of course, my sister and father roll their eyes at the idea when I share it with them at supper, but my aunt seems to smile at it. I could loose arrows from the ramparts and install some cannons. That will keep everyone away. I shall fashion it like High Sunderland Hall, one of the Priestley family's lavish homes; built like a fort, only in the middle of nowhere on the bare hillside. There are no castles or forts in this region, there has never been need of them. We are not on a route to anywhere and are surrounded by unnavigable hills. This region has been left alone, so lacks the history of battles and kings.

Shibden's roof is leaking again and the windows are draughty. Any plans I have drawn up for improvements seem too expensive. If only I had full ownership, I would forge ahead regardless. But in kindly including me in his inheritance, my uncle failed to give me the other two thirds of the income which would have made my life considerably easier. I must contend with my aunt and my father, who struggle to cope when I move a cushion. How will I ever make Shibden the Grand Hall or Castle it should be with only a third of the income?

I count my blessings that my uncle included me at all and I have some freedoms. As my father shows little interest in the estate, I have the freedom to make some changes here and there – but what I see is potential, a great deal of it, heading in two distinct directions; the potential to make more money from the land itself, and the potential to change the Hall for good. What I envisage, or should I say dream of, is parklands, a woodland walk, a lake at the bottom of the valley, a grand entrance, and once and for all to hide away the servants in passageways and tunnels. One cannot create the idea of grandeur to guests when the servants are marching back and forth in plain view.

The grand designs for little Shibden excite me, but their price takes the wind from my sails. I shall start small. I have restored the timber cladding to age the Hall again, increased the wooden wall panelling throughout. I have nearly convinced Father and Aunt that raising the ceiling and adding a staircase in the main hall will greatly improve it. I have more work to convince them yet. Without more money I cannot do much else for now.

Moreover, without more money I cannot travel again for a while. I enjoyed my time in Paris, but my friends have moved on and married. I'll visit again but it will never be the same. I think I need a big adventure. Something no one else has done; at least not someone from Halifax. I can be remembered as the Lister Explorer.

I find my well-thumbed atlas and open it on a random page. Russia.

Then I remember my poor flower, wilting just a few miles away. Can I really consider leaving her? Or must I wait for her to recover and join me? How much convincing will it take for her to come to Russia with me? It's taken several months just to get her to York. I decide I will give her a few more months; by my birthday in April I will decide our futures. Or rather, I will give her until then to decide to commit to me or not. If I am going to travel with a companion, I'd like at least to know privately that she is my wife.

Damn Mrs Ainsworth. Fancy falling out of a carriage.

Miss Walker

Miss Lister cannot stop me from crying and I tell her perhaps we should keep our friendship private, a secret even, but she will not hear of it. She gives me an ultimatum: unless I carry on as we were, she does not wish to see me. She tells me she will go travelling, on a two-year expedition, travelling all the way to Russia. Russia of all places! Why does she want to go to Russia? Why will she leave me?

She stands looking at me. Waiting for an answer. Miss Lister can be quite fearsome sometimes. She reminds me of someone else who looked at me like that once. I feel myself tremble. But she softens. Her face calms and she comes to sit next to me on the bed. She takes hold of one of my hands. She is so patient with me. She tells me not to fret and gives me until April to decide, but even April seems too soon. Then I realise that I need to tell her something. The reason I am so fearful, so doubtful, and it all finally comes tumbling out.

Miss Lister

She tells me something happened between her and Mr Ainsworth when she was just seventeen, just after he was married to her friend. She says she did not wish for it but poor innocent thing that she is, didn't realise until it was too late what his intentions were. Despite none of it being her fault, she takes the full weight of the guilt upon herself, as if she had sought out his attentions behind her friend's back. But from what she says, I think he contrived the whole situation. Saw an innocent young woman who could easily be taken advantage of. All I can do is sit and hold this naive and trusting young girl in my arms as she weeps and shakes and blurts out her account of him seducing her, though she barely understood what he was doing. I hear how he orchestrated an evening where the two were alone, and he gave her one too many glasses of wine and convinced her that it was not a sin to have a playful kiss. Then a playful touch of her neck, her back and her thighs. She had wanted to please and believed the way to make him stop was to show little resistance and hope it would end, and he would laugh and say he had just been teasing – but it did not end. He was not teasing.

When she tried to squirm free of him, he moved on top of her with her two hands in one of his, and his other hand pulled up her skirts. She screamed, she told me. At least she thought she had. But he had sent the servants away and

110

locked the doors. Her friend was asleep at the other end of the house. So she stopped screaming and blamed herself for allowing this to happen, for allowing him to think he could do this. She said to him, I hate you, and he replied that he did not care, and that no one would believe her. He would tell his wife that she seduced him, and she would lose her friendship forever and her reputation would be ruined; no one would ever marry her. Little Miss Walker believed him. And so she lay there looking at the ornate ceiling above her as he ruined the rest of her life.

Miss Walker

She was the first person I'd ever told.

I had always intended for Mrs Ainsworth to come alone to visit. So as not to arouse suspicion, I had written to beg her to come alone as I was unwell but wanted company. I hoped he would agree to it too, and then I would be alone with her, not to breathe a word about him, but to have my friend back, a chance for us to talk, remember our girlhoods.

But she is gone. At least she will never know about what happened. Selfishly, I felt some relief that I would never have to see him again. I believed it was all over and that I could finally carry on.

Only a second letter arrived just a few days after the first with his ugly writing on the front. I believed it would be about funeral arrangements, which it was, but it was a long letter, and in it he had the audacity to propose marriage to me. How could he? He ruined my one true friendship and could not even allow me to grieve for her. She is not even buried yet. How dare he!

Miss Lister held me for all the time I needed to cry and recover myself after receiving this letter. I hoped she understood some more of me now; why I feel at the mercy of others, so afraid of pleasure, deserving of nothing but a solitary life for what I have done. She tells me that I have done nothing, that it was all him. I try to believe her. Then she is exasperated with me, I can hear it in her voice. She moves away from me and paces, knowing there is nothing she can say to fix this.

I think she would shoot him dead if he showed up here. I think I would like that.

Miss Lister

That abomination of a man Mr Ainsworth has been writing each day now to beg Miss Walker to write back to him with a decision. His wife not even buried! Has he no guilty thoughts for what he has done? He simply thinks he can now claim her, again.

For some unimaginable reason she tells me she needs to think and will write back to him with her decision. As if there is any decision to be made! I am incensed and cannot hide it. She is now deciding between Mr Ainsworth and me.

I snatch from her a ridiculous six-page letter in which he exhorts that he has always loved her and is sorry he was so 'forthcoming' all those years ago. Forthcoming! He says he could not control himself around her. He'd married Mrs Ainsworth for money when they were both so young, but now he is free he wants nothing more than to marry Miss Walker. He goes on to say how he was there for her in the grief of her fiancé Mr Fraser and so she is in his debt! How was he there for her, I ask her?

She tells me he wrote several letters of condolence, which she burned in the fire and never replied to. I tell her he would have been pleased at Mr Fraser's death, leaving her still single and available for him in the future.

Then it strikes me. Could Mrs Ainsworth's accident have been planned? I do not mention this, of course.

It takes some time, but I believe she finally now sees him for the snake he is, sees him as I see him, and then she becomes woeful that she has been stupid and naive. I cannot say much on that point without offending her.

She allows me to write back to him on her behalf with a blunt no. Although I'd have chosen stronger language, I must make it sound like Miss Walker. She will not attend the funeral as it would be simply too difficult, both for her grief and her fear of seeing him. She, or rather I, ask him to leave her alone for good. I tell him she will burn any future letters and he had no right to do what he did then, or to propose to her now. It seems to be the end of the whole bother; if only she could erase him from her memory as easily.

On the day of poor Mrs Ainsworth's funeral, we go to our Parish Church and say our own prayers for her.

Since the sending of the letter, and thankfully no more arriving, Miss Walker slowly seems more emboldened and I tell her I will give her until summer, not April, when her strength will be back, for a decision on our commitment. I will not travel with her until I know for sure how she feels. We seal our agreement with a kiss; summer is the final time for her decision.

I say all this to her through smiles, but inside I am at a loss. This girl unhinges me when I see her. Come summer, I may have a lucky escape if she chooses 'no' and we will be done once and for all. I could set off into the world again. Perhaps I should have left the deadline at April after all and not let this drag on for too long.

Chapter Eleven

Spring, 1833: Another confession and another bout of melancholy

Miss Lister

It is my birthday night, the third of April. I am now forty-two years old. I never stood so alone. I am used and reconciled to my loneliness.

We had intimate relations in the Moss House again today. She had three long orgasms. We seem to be back on track these last few weeks and she says she cannot bear to be without me, yet she still harks on sometimes about it being wrong. However, she does not resist my caresses. This last week, despite it being my birthday, she is miserable again, as usual. The little thing has everything to be wished for but the power of enjoying it.

Miss Walker

I would be so lonely without her now. Miss Lister tells me she shall pass away like a meteor and leave no trace behind.

Miss Lister

I keep telling myself I do not care what she decides come summer, but when I lie with her in my arms, tears roll down my cheeks. I obviously care more for her than I imagined. Am I under her spell? To have this snatched away, what would I do next?

Miss Walker

I cannot give her a decision yet; she gave me until summer and I will not answer sooner, but I do swear to her that I will never marry.

Miss Lister

It wasn't the right moment to bring it up; after all, she was declaring that she would never marry, which could have just meant to a man but may have meant to either sex, but I quite like the idea of a wedding ceremony. I'll wait until her decision and if it's a yes, then damn it, we'll be married too.

Miss Walker

Without much suggestion from me, despite my hopes for it, it is she who proposes that we marry – each other. I say if we are to do it, it should be done properly, an unbreakable commitment. Perhaps that will set my mind at rest, if we commit in the sight of God. She assumes my answer come summer will be yes. Why wouldn't it be?

Miss Lister

She says if we were to marry it would need to be binding, the same as a marriage; we will declare on the Bible and take the sacrament together. A summer wedding.

Miss Walker

I wonder, if men are not allowed to be wed to each other and are even hung for it, then it must be the same between women?

Miss Lister

Someone has got into her head. She'll make herself ill again. I speak with authority to reassure her.

Miss Walker

She brings up Mr Ainsworth again. She wants me to say that it's not my fault, that I can move on, but the words do not come to me and I start to cry all over again, as if everything happened just yesterday rather than many years past.

Miss Lister

I have begun to lose respect for her. Can I honestly wait for the break of summer for a decision when it seems plain she can never decide? Thank God my mind is not like hers.

Miss Walker

Then she shakes me and looks me right in the eyes and says we all have our regrets and sorrows. We just have to live with them. I ask her what sorrows and regrets could the perfect Miss Lister ever have? And she replies, I killed a man.

Miss Lister

As soon as the words leave my mouth, I know it is not the sort of sentence you can retract. As Miss Walker sits there, her eyes red from the tears of her own sorrows, and her mouth now wide with shock, I know I must tell the truth as she has done. My confession has burned inside me. I haven't even committed it to my diary in my secret code, but now it has come tumbling out. With the saying of it, I selfishly feel some relief. But of all the people I could have shared it with, is meek little Miss Walker the one to tell something that could lead me to the gallows? But it is said now. I certainly have some explaining to do.

I pour us both a stiff drink and explain to her that I had wanted him dead but had not wished it to have happened. He was Shibden's groom and I had always argued with the man a great deal. He was constantly undermining me, questioning what I did, moaning when I asked him to do the very job I paid him for, belittling me in front of other staff. I should have had the courage to dismiss him or discuss him with Father, but the other staff all thought highly of him, as did Father. They never saw what he was like with me alone, how he looked at me with judgement in his eyes. As I was often away in France, I just hoped one day I would return and he would have moved on. But he never had.

It happened at Langton Hall when I was visiting Isabella and her family. Her brother was all set for a spot of shooting and, trying to be of use and not allowed to shoot myself, not through lack of skill or experience but through lack of invitation to join them, I ordered our groom up the tree to scare the crows. He protested but I was sick of him. I made him go up. I asserted my authority and threatened him with his job. I'd rather hoped he would refuse to climb up and just walk away. That was what I really wanted, for him to have walked away and I could have simply employed a new groom with no one any the wiser. It was my fault he was there when Mr Beech shot. Poor Mr Beech, the Norcliffes' long-serving groom, who was simply trying to scare some birds into flight, carries the full brunt of the blame; no one saw me near, but I was there when he fell. I saw him bloodied and crumpled at the base of the tree. When I heard the others running towards us, I ran and hid.

I felt guilty for Mr Beech who shot him, but I confess I was also relieved, and concerned that someone may have seen me argue with him just before. They hadn't though. No one was watching me. Or judging me. Except myself. And God.

I confess to her my fear of being charged. But how could I have known they would start shooting so soon? They have hanged people for much less, I tell her. The people of Halifax would bay for my blood, I'm sure. They'd bring back the gibbet specially to chop off my head. Who would testify on my behalf in a courtroom? Would they talk about my peculiarities? My fear is that if accused, anyone I'd ever met or who didn't like the cut of my jib would testify against me and I would not stand a chance. Even if found innocent, the accusation would ruin our family name, end our business, all the tenants would leave us; I would never truly be free again. It all pours out and she takes it in.

Am I glad he's dead, I wonder privately? Do I fear God's wrath on the matter? I am not sure He cares. Am I afraid I will be caught now that I have told Miss Walker? I certainly am.

While on the subject of telling the truth, seeing her fearful eyes on me and thinking that she may never speak to me again, I decide to tell her everything, for what have I to lose? If she may marry me and forfeit all others, then she needs to know what she is getting herself in to. I start from the beginning with Eliza. Then tell her, the first person I've ever shared it with, about my love for Mariana and how she broke my heart.

Miss Walker

What a pair we make. My perfect Miss Lister has her own secrets which she has revealed at last.

I knew she had other lovers before me. I wish she hadn't; I wish I had been her first. I had always imagined her so invulnerable, but to hear her speak of Mariana, I could tell her heart had been broken. I feel jealous of Miss Lister's love for her, but she seems to be reconciled to it now. She seems to have chosen me. How foolish I have been to keep her waiting. No wonder she has been so angry at my asking her to wait.

But to have led someone to their death and not told anyone! I am not as surprised as I should be. I have always slightly feared her. Does this repulse me, or attract me more? Does this make me as wicked? As complicit? Are there any sins left that we are not guilty of? Perhaps I need to steal something too, just to have done, as I'll end up in Hell regardless.

Chapter Twelve

Summer, 1833: A year on from the first kiss at Shibden

Miss Lister

Summer arrives, and I ask her plainly will she marry me? She says not yet, which I take as a no.

It is now a year since we first kissed at Shibden. A year of turmoil. A year that I have spent as a character in a novel whose life is turned this way and that with no care for my suffering, just others' amusement. I've told her everything about myself, held up my very heart for her to inspect and she rejects me.

I shall leave tomorrow. The Hall is in a fair state and the estate is in good hands. My aunt seems in reasonable health and has my father and sister to keep her company. If I do not leave soon, she will no doubt fall ill and take a few years to die and all the time I will be stuck here wishing that I'd left when I had the chance. How awful of me to think this way, but I am driven to it. A year of my life I have waited. Wasted. My heart has been in joy and sadness and now falls into a melancholy I do not recognise. I have caught it from her. Her uncertainty, her fear of the future. Damn her. I will leave tomorrow.

There is another thing I must do before I leave, something which has played on my mind since I confessed it: I need to make right with Mr Beech. The poor fellow shoulders all the guilt for the death of our groom, but half the burden is mine. I shall seek him out at Langton Hall to make my peace with him. Though neither of us can be truly forgiven, to share our load may ease our minds. I hate the thought of it, but my mind is made up. I have guilt enough for the dead man, but to feel guilty for a man who lives when it can be amended is foolish. I was informed by Isabella that it was deemed an accident and that they paid our dead groom's family handsomely. I shall put my fate in the hands of Mr Beech. Prison or the gallows may await. It will be some good gossip for Halifax.

If I am still a free woman, I will then call in on Mariana. It's been too long, I find myself missing her. I wonder if I should tell her of the turmoil which has vexed me this past year? Will we laugh together at how I could have been so duped?

Shall I tell Miss Walker all this? Shall I tell her that her decision is 'no' and I am going to see my former love? That would be cruel. I shall tell her simply that I am heading for London and do not know how long I will be gone. I may venture farther. She'd hoped I'd put down roots here and would just wait for her forever. Instead, we shall part as friends and I shall see where I find her when I return. What care I?

My aunt tells me she is sad to see me go just a year after my return, and especially so quickly. I tell her I want to make good time for London and if she feels well enough then she and Marian shall journey down to join me in a few weeks before I travel farther. I rather like the idea of them joining me in London and even Marian seems to think it is a good idea. I suggest she could even then cross the Channel with me to re-visit France.

I make Marian swear to write to me should Aunt's health fail and I must return in haste. I would rather be here to say farewell, even if it is a false call, than to miss her.

Miss Walker

She made the decision for me. After a year of waiting, she said it was no longer fair. If she'd been a male suitor, she would not have been made to wait half so long for a reply. She reminds me she is twelve years my senior and that all the travels she aims to undertake cannot wait. I had thought that she was settled now at Shibden with all her talk of plans for it, but I suppose they were to occupy her mind while she waited for my decision, and now that she has made it, all that is cast aside and off she goes.

I cannot stay here without seeing her each day, without the Moss House to retreat to, without being in her arms. It is all my fault. I have lost her. Even if I recant and declare a 'yes', she will not accept it now. I have missed my opportunity.

I cannot be alone here so I write to my sister to ask if I can join her as soon as they can send the carriage. I want to see what her life has become, see her children, my nieces and nephew. I shall throw myself into their lives and find joy in their company. I shall stay indefinitely with them as a family. No more lonely old Crow Nest for me. I shall away from here. If I cannot be with Miss Lister and her family, then I shall find my own family again.

I want to see Marian and ask her thoughts and keep up our friendship, but Miss Lister will be there. I send her a note inviting her to visit me and hope sincerely that she comes.

Miss Lister

One can never leave as quickly as one wants. I had to order horses and let Isabella and Mariana know to expect me and await their replies to confirm they would be home. I had to book lodgings on the way down and find a room to rent in London. I then had to write ahead to friends there, giving them the address to reply to.

Finally, a week later, I am packed and ready to go. My aunt cries and even Marian looks sad, but they assure me they will make the trip down to visit me soon. My sister ventures so far as to say she may come by herself if Aunt isn't up to it, which pleases me, and I insist she does. London will be a marvel to her, Paris too, if she's brave enough to join me. She has not been there in many years. I promise to look after her and we say goodbye fondly, as sisters should, and I feel guilty for leaving and always being so harsh on her.

My father bids me farewell and asks again if all the business is well cared for. I reassure him it is in safe hands with our steward and there is nothing he need do except support his decisions. He asks me quietly if I am seeing the lovely Mariana on my journey down and I reply yes, and he winks. He always makes me feel awkward about it, so I blush and rush into the carriage. With a wave of my hand I leave their lives behind, head from Shibden's courtyard and up the track to the main Halifax road, past the spot where one day I plan to build a gatehouse, and turn right towards York.

At the last minute, I decide to call in at Crow Nest to say farewell. She meets me on the doorstep reluctantly like a petulant child. She barely looks at me as I tell her to be strong and look after herself. She tells me she is going to see her sister and I promise that we will travel together next time, that I will not be gone long. We can write all the time. But even as I say it, I know it is not true. I am heading off to see Mariana and intend to take pleasure with her. Familiar, passionate pleasure with my former lover and with Isabella too, possibly. I do not know how long I will be gone or even if I will return. I say I will write but I do not know if I wish to. I will leave her. If she cannot commit to me then she has lost me, and she can see how it feels to be left alone. I kiss her on both cheeks politely and let go of her hands. She does not look at me.

So fly away, little broken bird. I cannot save you or fix you; the only one who can do that is yourself. You are not my kin, my wife, or even my lover any more. I will leave you here in your sad memories and hope that your sister can pluck you from this melancholy as I have tried to and failed.

Farewell Miss Walker. I am better off without you.

Miss Walker

I want to fall at her feet, beg her to stay, but I remain dumb. I understand her leaving me, I truly do. It just feels so cruel. But then, it is cruel of me to expect her to stay. A year since she first swept into my life and for a year I have kept her on a thread. Now she takes the scissors and cuts it and I am left, lifeless.

My sister has sent the carriage to collect me. I do not have long before it arrives. How simple it would have been, already packed and dressed, to have climbed into the carriage with Miss Lister instead. To have decided that I would go with her down south and not up to Scotland where my sister waits. I could at any moment have said, let me go with you, and I'm sure she would have accepted. I would now be sitting next to her, my arm in hers, riding southwards on an adventure together. Instead I stand here on the doorstep, alone. Always to be alone. I stand here until the carriage arrives from my sister, not moving, lost in my thoughts. I have missed my opportunity. Again. I have let her drive off without me.

I step up into Sutherland's empty carriage and am whisked northwards to the cold, to my sister. Yes, I want to see her, but her husband will be there, and they will make me socialise and try to pair me off with someone a long way from home.

The servants probably thought me mad, standing there on the doorstep. I knew I could not go back into the house after she left as I would have run into my room and locked the door and never left. So, I stood there and waited, and eventually boarded this carriage instead. I am a prisoner now, being transported to Scotland as punishment. A prisoner in my own life. A prisoner in my indecision. I think about the joy on my sister's face, the little ones who will grow to know me and love me as their aunt. I have chosen my family over Miss Lister's. Youth over age. I just hope I can bring them some happiness.

Farewell Miss Lister. You are better off without me.

Chapter Thirteen

Summer, 1833: A journey in opposite directions

Miss Lister

At Langton Hall I told him directly, the guilt is not yours alone, it was my fault also. I might as well tell you, for if it should reduce your grief then that will be a good outcome. I've carried the grief of it myself and realised it was unfair of me not to tell you. I hope you can forgive me.

Mr Beech looked at me and seemed surprised, but then I saw relief creep in. I wondered for a moment if it would turn to anger, but he simply shook my hand, tutted quietly and then walked away. I could have lain down on the ground with the relief of it.

It became a week of confessions. After leaving Langton Hall and the Norcliffes behind me after a few days of catching up, reminiscing, and a pleasurable fumble with Isabella for old time's sake, I head over to Lawton Hall in Cheshire to see its mistress, Mariana.

No sooner had I told her about the Langton Hall incident and how relieved I felt to have finally spoken with Mr Beech, than Mariana was itching to tell me something herself. I think she felt guilty at her choice over the years, her naive hope that Charles would not live long, but it turns out that there was another reason that she left me. She wants to tell me so I will not continue to think that it was due to a personal shortcoming of mine. She reassures me that I am perfect and was all she ever wanted, except – and she lands a heavy blow – that I could never give her a child.

The still childless Mariana stares at me with her wide beautiful eyes and I see this has burned away in her since she married Charles over fifteen years ago. She hasn't told me before because she'd hoped it would happen for her, she tells me. Then it would have been self-evident. However, many years later, childless, for her to voice that this is what she wanted all this time, opens up a grief for what she has not been blessed with. From Miss Walker's grief to Mariana's, I seem to be the one others cry on at the moment.

I can see from her tears how much she wanted a child and to be denied the one thing that would have justified her decision, fifteen years of putting up with Charles, of breaking her own heart by leaving me, seems cruel. She cries as if she has actually lost a child. I imagine it is the idea of it, of what could have been, that grieves her. She sobs that if she'd had one straight away, when Charles used to take his pleasure with her regularly, the child would be fifteen years old, an individual learning their place in the world, talking to us now, looking like a young version of her.

For years she lay with him purely so that she may conceive, she confesses. I had thought it had just been on occasion to keep him happy. I knew she was having intimate relations with him regularly enough as he gave her, and in turn me, gonorrhoea. We would still meet regularly over the years after they wed, and I believe he knew what we got up to. He had affairs too, hence the disease, but they still tried, or at least she tried to conceive, and she allowed him to pleasure himself with her. In return he was happy to finance Mariana's life and travels, often with me.

I passed the disease onto Isabella too, but I never told Mariana that. I couldn't just be at her whim all the time, ready to lift my skirts at any time she wanted. Once Isabella realised I'd been with someone else, whom she rightly assumed was Mariana, that was it for us for many years, until I won her over once more. Charles' indiscretion cost me a great deal of pleasure, and some awkward visits to the doctor and expensive treatments that have never worked. I believe he knew he'd given it to us both – he probably revelled in it. It was his small way of showing a power over me too. He probably contracted it on purpose.

I wonder if the reason for her telling me about this longing for a child is that now she has given up. We are the same age, after all, and with nothing left for Charles to offer her and no sign of him dying soon, does she want to start up with me again? I try to ignore this thought as my hopes are so quickly dashed by her, but I do wonder, though I do not ask outright.

I stay with her for a few more days and when she talks of Halifax, she lets something slip and I realise she has heard of Miss Walker and me. Though I have not made anything more than a passing reference to her as an acquaintance, Mariana mentions my Moss House, which only my aunt or Mrs Priestley could have told her about. I wonder if it has made her jealous.

Finally, as it is a season of confessions, I tell her all about Miss Walker. It is done with now, so what have I to lose? I recount

Mrs Priestley's dramatic exit from Crow Nest and seemingly our lives, and Mariana laughs, as I did, but appreciates the loss of a friend. Would Mrs Priestley ever imagine that myself and Mariana were just as close? Probably not. She only saw us together on occasional visits as we tended to travel together or meet elsewhere; Mariana was never a permanent part of Shibden or Halifax life. She never wanted to be. Miss Walker, on the other hand, was in the centre of it all, somehow related to every other person in Halifax. We both feel sad after all our confessions, but neither has a solution for the other. She does not ask me to take up with her again. We do not even kiss. We are both alone.

To be condemned to a life alone over a potential child! I wouldn't want the worry, the constant fear for them; so few survive to adulthood. What if you do not even like them? Or they kill you on the way out? I do not see the appeal.

Miss Walker

Within the day I am in love with them all, the three little babes. I want them for myself but am glad at least that they are related so I can have some small claim on them. They have the Walker colourings that my sister and I share: golden hair, pale skin and a small splattering of freckles, as if added as an afterthought. Elizabeth has raised them well; they are calm and smile readily. They are content and interested and after just one day the two little toddlers come to me and laugh and let me hold them; Mary and George. The baby Elizabeth lies happily in my arms gazing up at me with her wide bright eyes. I imagine she wonders how I can look like her mother but be different somehow. I could take the children out without Elizabeth and anyone would assume they were mine. I would give anything to walk into the town with baby Elizabeth in my arms and hear people coo over her and smile at me over what I have produced.

The weather is warmer than I thought. We sit outside and take the carriage to the coast and I see the sea, the wonderful ocean stretching before me, the sounds of waves I have not heard since I was a child, so much more reassuring and welcoming than the sounds of the winds and trees blowing back at home. I could sit for hours watching the little ones on the sands, the baby asleep in her cot, talking easily and freely with my sister as if we have never been apart. She gives me a pile of novels to indulge in and I feel alive, awake and content. I have almost forgotten my need for Miss Lister.

Weeks pass in our tranquillity with the children, breakfasts, lunches, reading, sewing, receiving visitors. Elizabeth updates me with what she hears from family in Yorkshire, often about me. I do not tell her anything at first, I just laugh at the gossip and respond to any references to Miss Lister with my well-rehearsed line: she was just a new acquaintance. Past tense.

Then Sutherland returns from his business down in London and bursts through our quietude. She reassures me he is only to be home a short while, but all of us are tense around him, almost not daring to be in the same room or breathe loudly in his presence. He asks rude questions such as why am I not married yet, what am I doing with the estate, have I written my will and what's this I hear about a Gentleman Jack of Halifax? It takes all my strength not to be cold towards him but to answer courteously, not to let the children see that I am as afraid of him as their mother is. Elizabeth must be always on guard; most days, he strides in at an unpredictable hour without a word, his intentions clear, and she rises and goes with him to their bedroom, leaving me with the children and the nanny. She comes down a short while later and acts as if she just went to read him some poems, but she then holds the children closely as if they give her strength.

Thankfully after just a week he leaves again, seemingly keen to get back down to London for business. He seems bored by life here and anxious to return to his gentlemen's clubs. He tells us he has seen boxing in the capital and is supporting one of the fighters. Later, Elizabeth reassures me he will be gone for a month this time. It takes a few days for us to really believe he is gone and not jump at every opening door, but slowly we relax, the children brighten, the servants are less skittish and visitors begin to arrive again.

For every happiness, God gives unhappiness. As if each pleasure must be paid for. The more pleasure taken, the more punishment received. She tells me she is happy with the ratio of time with just her and the children and occasional visitors against the time he is home and is, as she says, demanding. I wonder how she can suffer it. Any time my face reveals my true thoughts – why on God's Earth did you marry him? – she tuts at me and says I know, I know, I should have listened to you and John. Then she looks at the three children and we both realise they are worth every suffering a person could endure.

Another few weeks pass and I feel settled, ready to stay for a long time, perhaps forever. I have my room set up as I like it with items from home, and more of my clothes have arrived from Crow Nest and some of my books for Elizabeth. We spoil ourselves and buy a copy of a book each, so we can read them at the same time and pause and comment and discuss each chapter. We are inseparable. She is my best friend, and how I could ever be apart from her again I do not know. I will stay here and be part of their lives and watch these children grow, even if it means having to stand by when Sutherland strides in and, as Elizabeth says, asserts that he is the man of the house.

He is home again. He does not like me. He tries to belittle me in front of the children, far too young to care, but it hurts me. I wonder what it will be like when they are older? Will they agree with their father that I am meek and should have wed and am, as he says, selfish to sit on a fortune and not share it with a worthy man and children of my own? I spend some of it on Elizabeth and the children in secret. We tell him all the new books, threads and matching shawls were mine already, but one day he sees a bill in amongst Elizabeth's letters which he opens and reads and shouts at us both as if we are mere children. I say it is my money to spend as I choose and he throws one of the books, which I was only halfway through reading, into the fire. I notice he is wearing a new waistcoat and in a moment of boldness comment that we have our books from my half of the Walker estate whilst he has his waistcoat from Elizabeth's. I can see him boil inside and without a word he seizes Elizabeth roughly and takes her upstairs. I sit and wait anxiously with the children for what seems like a lifetime for her to return.

We promise each other we will be more secretive in future and I swear to her I will never answer back to him again. What has my dear Elizabeth ever done to deserve this? I realise that if I stay here there will be no end to this, his coming and going. He already treats me with contempt as if I am his second wife, as if he can treat me just like her and try to control me, ignoring that I am a guest and have as much wealth and probably more status than him. He sees me just as a woman, beneath him in all ways.

If I remain here, I will be accepting of him just as Elizbeth was so innocently five years ago. Despite vowing to never marry and managing without it thus far, to live here with my sister would be as good as marrying Sutherland myself. She is trapped. I realise I should take heed of my own warning and that if John were alive, he too would say the same. My presence here may alleviate her suffering while he is away but cannot solve it and may make it worse if he resents us. My poor sister is legally bound to him forever and he can do with her as he pleases. He may have one Walker in his clutches, but he shall not have me too. I will not let him decide my fate as I am still free.

He leaves again and thankfully is gone for two months, during which time Elizabeth realises she is with child again.

Chapter Fourteen

Winter, 1833: A journey overseas and a surprise reunion

Miss Lister

I leave Mariana full of discontent. How she vexes me! Why are women so complicated? They fill me with half-truths and suggestions and never a plain answer, and I always get hurt. Mariana will not leave Charles but I cannot have an affair with her, so I am once again single and left waiting for him to die. I should orchestrate a need for him to climb up a tree during a shoot.

I had come all the way over the country, far out of my way heading to London, in the hope of either an ending and a goodbye or a reunion and a new beginning, and at least some pleasure. I had left Miss Walker behind and now want to leave Mariana, thus freeing me up for new adventures and diary pages to fill with life in London, Paris and beyond.

Instead my mind races and I wonder if Miss Walker is succumbed to the same longing for a child as Mariana? Is that what created such indecision that she would even consider the bastard Mr Ainsworth, purely for the child he could offer her? Is the sad truth of it that I can never truly satisfy either of them without impregnating them? What a pair they make! I should find some orphans, scrub them up and present them one each with a bow on top. Give them a better life of smothering mothers' love. Girls, definitely girls for them both.

Now free of these two women and some of the guilt over a man's death, the city awaits with better, more constant friends than those I leave behind. Once in London I visit my aristocratic friends, including Vere and her new baby. She seems happier than I ever knew her to be when we were younger and single, out and about in society. She was always awaiting marriage and the life she now has. Her whole existence was centred on it. I was just a companion, a distraction for her while she waited, and then she secured a husband, became a Lady and now has a perfect baby, which even I think is charming.

Have I been delusional all these years, all my life, that a woman could ever be satisfied with me? That I alone would be enough? Just my love, all of it, a dedication of my life to theirs, a marriage even, security, the freedom to be themselves, nothing more and nothing less? Will they become full of regrets with hindsight, as Miss Walker may be in another ten years when she too may be childless still? By then will it be too late? It is too late for Mariana, it is too late for both of them, for they have broken my heart and chosen something that does not exist over any happiness I could give them, and the result is we are all unhappy. Not one of us has taken a gamble and won.

After a few weeks in London I am left feeling inadequate. After all my visits, it becomes clear that I have nothing to share with my friends, I have achieved nothing this past year. I talk of my plans for improvements to Shibden but nothing has happened yet, and without Miss Walker I'll barely have the funds. I talk of future travel but what of it? I have not achieved anything, it is all just talk. They are not interested in my coal mines and Halifax politics; it is just a small town they've never seen in the inconsequential North, without a gallery or museum to its name. I feel lowly in their company.

I wait in London for my aunt and Marian to agree to visit but they do not. They prattle on in their letters filled with excuses. I send a note to Marian to say I will wait two more days to hear from her and should very much like her to accompany me to Paris. I wait three days and receive no reply, so book myself onto the crossing and head down to the coast without her. Why will she not come? I could do with some company, even hers. She needs to leave Shibden and Halifax some time or other. I wonder if perhaps she has met someone in my absence? Or is that rather far-fetched? I realise it was ten years ago that Marian and Father last came to Paris. My memory may not be perfect but I'm sure we enjoyed ourselves. If only I had my diary from the time to consult – but they are all safely tucked away back at Shibden.

I immerse myself in travel; it is my only pleasure left, it seems. I arrive in Paris and stay in rooms I have used before and re-visit my familiar haunts. I walk over the grand bridges, go to the galleries and museums and marvel at the peculiarities deemed worthy of immortality, of reflecting cultures which are now lost, of reminding us of the Earth's journey through time and how fleeting our own existence is. I eat and drink more than my fill and buy gifts to send back to Aunt and Marian to show them what they are missing. A rare good fortune crosses my path as an old acquaintance introduces me to a lady from the Danish Court who invites me to Copenhagen. I do not hesitate to accept her offer. I will be an English novelty for her to show off to her friends, no doubt. The next moment we are on a ship again and I am presented at the Danish Court!

It is enjoyable but solitary in Denmark. I do not speak the language well and being an English novelty leaves me feeling disheartened. I am not heard of. If only I had a title! 'Miss' only gives away my singleness. I dream of introducing myself as Doctor Lister, but it is just that: a dream. I am introduced to so many people, but which of them will I ever really know, will ever know me? Which of them could become part of my life forever?

At parties and dinners I talk with ladies whose English is clear and crisp, and they struggle to understand me. Though I've spent my life avoiding a Yorkshire accent, it creeps in at the corners and muffles some of my words; I must work hard to enunciate, my humour is lost to them and I seem dull and uneducated. I can see them comment on my clothing which feels well-worn and shabby next to theirs and even when I wear a new dress to attend Court, one which is not black, a fact which somewhat pains me but was worth a try, I still feel an outsider; even in beige.

I smile at women who would normally come to talk and raise a glass with me, intrigued by an English lady – but those younger than me do not seem to be interested. I stare at my reflection and I seem older, more tired, less alive. No wonder I have not met a lover here; I am no longer in my twenties. I am an old spinster, past her prime, older than the mothers of some of the girls I like the look of, and they all ask me, where is my husband? Am I a widow? They do not understand I have chosen this life, that I may have more interest in them than they can imagine, that I could give them more pleasure than they could dream of or will ever receive from their husbands. I have wasted my attractive years courting the wrong women and am now too old for those available. If only one of our York set had been right for me. If only Mariana... and I go over the same old ground. Reminiscing and regretting what could have been and never was to be. What use is regret? I cannot change anything.

There are so many paths in life we make for ourselves, but the two vital ones, our status and our love, are ordained for us. We are born as we are born, into whatever form God deems us worthy of. We are teased with and denied love regardless of our own capacity to love and be loved. Those who are most deserving of love seem least likely to be rewarded with it.

You cannot choose when and whom you love. Miss Walker treated it as a practical decision she needed to make, but when true love occurs, surely there is no decision? Just two people drawn together, whether the situation is right or wrong, whether their sex is a match or not; where there is love, true love, it must be so.

My money runs low as this extravagant trip and fine rooms and my new dress have been costly, and my diary reads woefully despite the foreign shores and new experiences. I feel as if I have seen it all before. I am not excited by it. Perhaps I need to go farther afield to really interest me again, avoid these modern cities which all seem similar to each other, with the same sorts of restaurants, theatres, dance halls, hotels; the carriages are the same, even fashions are similar and still fail to interest me.

I feel like a cork floating on the surface of the sea, unanchored, directionless; I can no longer see the coastline. I no longer know which way is home.

Would it be different if I were not alone? Would this be better if I had someone to share it with? It seems I am collecting experiences just to fill my diary, which may never be read, or shared, or appreciated. I long for someone to join me, not just for this trip, but for my life. If I am not to be blessed with love, then surely I cannot also be cursed to be left alone for the rest of my life as well? I need a companion.

Miss Walker

Like a ghost that will not leave me in peace, Mr Ainsworth rears his ugly head again. He has the audacity to write to my brother-in-law, the equally intolerable Sutherland, recommending he suggest I take him up on his proposal. The snake! Of course, both my sister and Sutherland are naive about him and think it a wonderful idea, but the letter, and Sutherland's menacing idea to read it aloud at dinner with guests, makes me flee from the room. Men are so cruel, doubly so Mr Ainsworth and Sutherland! Where can I go in the world to be protected from them, away from their gaze and meddling intentions?

My sister knows there is more to my reaction. She does not press the matter, but a week passes before Sutherland gives us any privacy. Finally, with the children in bed and the two of us alone, I tell my sister what happened when I was seventeen. When I told Miss Lister she was angry, but she did not know me at that time; for my sister, it brings back memories and explains why she had to see me in such a state. She tells me I should have told her, that she would have understood, she would have protected me, and after much apologising and sobbing, we swear to tell each other everything from now on. After imagining what has gone on these last five years in this house, we are up all night as she tells me what it has been like; nothing is secret between us any more. Except, of course, my true relations with Miss Lister. For why need I tell her of that? Miss Lister is gone from my life forever.

Sutherland harks on about the proposal until we bravely tell him that Mr Ainsworth was indiscreet when he was married. Sutherland does not look up from his plate. I tell him Ainsworth has no money of his own. Sutherland just grunts, the irony no doubt lost on him. My sister then states the case, which was our plan to tell him all along, that if I were to remain unmarried, my half of the estate will go to his children in due course. Sutherland perks up at this thought and looks at me for a while. He says, you really do not want to marry do you, little Walker? I meet his gaze and firmly reply that I do not. A few days later, he tells us he has sent a letter to Mr Ainsworth and that we will not hear from him again. I dread to think what he wrote of me.

The feeling in the house grows ever more intolerable. I love my sister and the children dearly, but my nerves are in shreds and I jump at every sound. He comes and goes more often now and treats me as another wife or servant, just as I thought he would. He barks at me to move things, fetch things, pour tea, pick up or quieten a child. He comments on my clothing and whether I look pale, which is most of the time. He tells us to leave him alone and then to keep him company. He grunts that he hopes the next child is another boy, for he does not want a houseful of women getting under his feet. I do not want to leave Elizabeth, especially as she's having another child, but after ten months with them, hoping and hoping that it would work out, she cuts me free.

One day, after two weeks in his ominous presence, never a moment alone with each other, I open my book and find a note: 'Go home to C. N. and we will visit you soon. I've loved having you here these months, but he was not your choosing, you should not suffer, one of us should be free. I love you, E.'

Miss Lister

I rise each day and walk the streets of Copenhagen as if they will give me an answer, or at least another chance meeting to lead me on to my next adventure. I turn the pages of an atlas and plot routes, but never choose one to follow. I decline invitations as I realise I have become a burden of a guest with little to say for myself.

Thankfully, after ten long months a letter arrives, which, although bad news, draws me from my stalemate and forces my next move. Marian's letter had been sent ten days before. Aunt is ill and I should return. I need no excuse and suddenly fall to action, and within the day I am on the coach heading back to the port. It will be a long journey home but at least I am heading somewhere, even though it is backwards. I am moving again and the journey and worry for my aunt occupy my mind. After all, in my present lonely state of mind, I might as well try to make a life for myself back in Shibden rather than be stuck in a rut here.

Miss Walker

We part with sorrow; all I want is for her to come with me, more than anything in the world, but she cannot leave him. She says she will try to visit often with the children, without him. Crow Nest will be our sanctuary. I have the address of a close friend of hers whom she visits each week to whom I can send more personal letters, and she will post me letters from Elizabeth without Sutherland reading them first. We can write freely again at least.

I cry and cry and thank God that he isn't here to see it. I leave when he is away as he may object to seeing his children's inheritance leave when he thought he had gained control over the entire Walker clan.

I cry all the long journey home, thinking of how it could have been, the sorrow of being away from her, the children and what she endures. But she is right. I should go home again to Crow Nest and try to make some life for myself there.

Miss Lister

I arrive back in December, just before Christmas. They are surprised to see me and after all my worrying and weeks at sea in stormy weather, my aunt is as fit as a fiddle. Marian apologises profusely – her second letter of reassurance must have missed me, but never mind, I am quite glad to be home. I remember last year's Christmas and wonder how a whole year could have passed and here we all are again, reunited. I take my usual tour of the grounds to see what has changed in these months of absence when I see someone in the distance walking towards Shibden. I know who it is straight away. Miss Walker.

Miss Walker

Marian Lister and I kept up our correspondence and I visit more regularly since my return from Scotland. I decided to pursue my friendship with her as she seems a good match; she is nearer my age than most of my family and acquaintances and is single too. We get along well and have decided we will travel to York for a short stay soon. I enquired last week if she'd heard from her sister on her travels and she told me that their aunt was taken ill a month ago, and as she had sworn to her sister that she would tell her if she needed to return, she'd written to her. She had then sent a second letter two days later to say that the worst had passed and she need not return, but she had had nothing in reply to either letter. I asked her if she was worried at not having heard from her and she replied that when she was

144

in France, they did not hear from her for weeks or months at a time. Did she never wish to join her, I ask, and she confides in me that she has been seeing someone, so does not want to leave. She makes me swear not to tell anyone.

Today it is my turn to visit Marian and I decide to walk over to Shibden rather than take the carriage. I'm feeling stronger and despite the cold chill, I encourage myself to accomplish the hour's walk. I am sure to be offered a lift home in the Lister carriage.

Then I see her. Plain as day. Miss Lister.

Chapter Fifteen

Spring, 1834: A marriage and a new addition to the Lister clan

Miss Lister

We shall henceforth call each other by our Christian names; it's a shame we have the same one! The only difference is that her name does not have an 'e' like my Anne. I'm rather accustomed to thinking of her as Miss Walker but I shall endeavour to call her Ann.

She should really be Mrs Anne Lister. I should be Mr Lister. I could even be Mr Lister-Walker to give myself some additional airs and graces. Only in private, of course.

I am wed. Again.

Clearly, Miss Walker, or rather Ann, need never know she is technically not my first wife. How awful of me to have married before! I wonder if I need some sort of official annulment – but then it is all a fiction in truth. A good fiction that makes us feel bound and committed and hopefully blessed by God in our union. It is a wonderful secret that is ours alone. She is my wife!

We chose Ann's favourite little church in York, Holy Trinity. We exchanged vows in our rooms and then went to church to take the sacrament together.

Now secured as my wife, she has agreed to move in permanently to Shibden and my family all approve, though hers do not, but never mind them – she will be away from them now.

When I saw her again after all those months apart, I knew what her answer should be. She was surprised to see me too, out on the point where our lands touch, and as we embraced, I felt at home. I can only imagine she felt the same as she cried, we both did in fact, and in hurried words we agreed to be together. It was silly to be separate when we were both single and alone. It seemed our months apart had done the trick to convince her and there was no hesitation in her answer. We walked back to Shibden together to tell the others that Miss Walker wished to move in with us.

My aunt, the only one aware of how tumultuous our relationship had been, replied that if we were both happy, then she was happy too.

My sister beamed with delight; it seems the two have become better acquainted in my absence, and Father welcomed her wholeheartedly and commented that he has put up with three single women in the house for years, so why not four?

Ann officially takes the room next to mine, which is connected by a servant's passageway at the back so no one need ever suspect we share our new bed each night, arm in arm in my little bedroom on the warm side of the Hall. It is nothing compared to the salubrious quarters she is used to, but she tells me she feels at home here and would not change it for the world.

She visits Crow Nest each week and still meets visitors there. I simply call in. It is easier to make it seem as though she still lives there. Her letters still go there and nothing else seems to change, other than the feeling in my heart that I am complete once more, with someone in my arms each morning and night who loves me and says she will be by my side forever.

How could I ever have imagined that contentment would be found just a few miles from my home, or that it would take so long to achieve it? Yet here we are; what is easily won could never feel as rewarding as this.

Miss Walker

I cannot imagine gaining pleasure with anyone but a woman now. There are no expectations of entering you, pushing you open; the pleasure is on the surface until you allow it to course through you. You are not thrust about. It is about all of your body, each part of it aroused in turn until you are hot and your down-there throbs for satisfaction. She is slightly larger than me, stronger, but her form does not threaten me. She may hold me down but she will let go at the asking, she may scratch me but never too hard, she may push herself against me but I do the same to her, I throw myself upon her, allow all my weight to press her down, I squeeze her close to me, wrap her in my arms.

The clean lines of her form, all pink flesh except the fine soft hair on her legs and special place and tucked underneath her arms; all mine for touching, kissing, caressing. I cannot believe I resisted her for so long. I think back on all those months when all I let her do was grope around and play with her fingers and tongue on me when there is so much more.

Our marriage helps and the privacy of our Moss House. She can own me now. I have given every inch of myself to her and want her to take it. I own her too; the shape of her is all mine to trace with my fingers, admire, adore. I learn from her how she touches me, squeezes my shoulders and arms, sucks my fingers and toes, gently unpins my hair and pulls out my curls until it all is free and wild and falls down my back and she slowly wraps it around her hand and pulls me close to her and kisses me, holding me against her. I explore her down-there and discover the taste of it and how to tease her, build her up, then finish her and make her call out in pleasure. Then we lie there, our arms entwined, our bodies touching as much as they can and were it not for my paler skin it would be hard to know where her body ends and mine begins.

Miss Lister

I lie staring at her golden hair and pale skin, with just enough freckles to accentuate her beautiful face. Her arms and legs are less firm than my own which have been strengthened by so much walking over the years, but hers are beautiful nonetheless, and they are all mine to touch and hold as I please.

She can be soft and passionate, and now as my wife, she allows me all of herself, and I to her; my body is hers. Since her liberation, she has become a surprisingly accomplished lover who takes her time over me and builds me up slowly, working on each part of me, kissing and caressing, kissing and caressing, then she gives me pleasure but keeps me waiting, as she returns to kissing, then caressing my breasts and squeezing my thighs and then she returns to my down-there and with her powerful mouth draws from me an orgasm which makes me call out her name, and then it is her turn for pleasure and we alternate until we are exhausted or gently fall into a slumber in each other's arms in the sanctuary of our private place, nestled in the woods, with high windows that no one can see into and a large wooden door, locked against the world as summer approaches.

Miss Walker

For all this pleasure my punishment is the Clap. She tells me it is manageable but I'm angry she did not warn me of this sooner. My down-there had become another of my worries these last few months and now I learn it is not my fault at all. Anne educates me and diminishes the magic of our pleasures somewhat by showing me a book of anatomy with diagrams that I'd rather not have seen. I shall accept it as a punishment for wanting her, desiring her.

It is still more that I could have imagined, this love we have, this freedom to just be. I have no barriers to her now. I strip down before her and allow her to claim all of me and I have a trust in her that I have never felt for anyone; I am safe, I am aroused. Her soft kisses all over me, that even when firm do not scare me but arouse me further. Each time our lovemaking is different; she focusses on a different place, keeping me guessing where she will caress me next. It is different kissing to a man's, which is always intent on the same end. All their words, hand holding, flattery, kisses, wandering hands, all of it on target for one thing: to penetrate you, to claim you for their own pleasure, as if accomplishing you, with no cares for your desires. To pierce you with their wildness and leave their seed inside you, to claim your body and your soul as theirs. I think of all the women throughout the world submitting, believing that it is God's choice for them – but He also gave us our own pleasure. Never written down by man, but passed on by women; a secret, never uttered or recorded, that we do not need men for true pleasure.

As I spend more time at Shibden, I am encompassed into the Lister fold. I had been so nervous that they would resent my presence, but they are a generous folk, so different from how Anne described, or rather bemoaned them to me. From all she had told me, I had grown to dread their reception – but I imagine we are all guilty of retelling the worst aspects of a person as they have riled us, forgetting the rest of the time when they are perfectly pleasant human beings.

My presence gives them an excuse to recount old stories, long told and heard over, but fresh to my ears. I hear of the tomboy Anne and how Marian would follow her around. Her father speaks of Samuel, her brother lost like mine, whom she had only mentioned in passing to me, but I hear that they were close. Marian tells me how jealous she was when Anne and Samuel would disappear for hours on end on their horses; she was never invited. Anne brushes it off, saying that Marian was not as strong on a horse, but I can tell that it was because Anne wanted her brother to herself, as I did mine.

Her father tells me of the letters he would receive from Anne's schools asking him to come and remove her, but he would reply that if they were incapable of teaching an intelligent young woman then they should not call themselves teachers and should quit the profession altogether, and we all laugh.

Her aunt tells me in private how Anne has given her life such joy. She describes her as peculiar but enchanting, and I like this summary. Her aunt never wanted to marry either and her brother had always promised that he would look after her and she need never settle for anyone unless she loved them – and she never loved anyone other than her family. She was bold at courting and parties and social gatherings but never met her match in a man and in time slipped into the easy and secluded daily life of Shibden. She tells me that she and Anne's uncle were already quite old when Anne moved in with them, so Anne never saw her in her prime. It had taken some convincing for young Anne to take her aunt to Paris with her but they both recount it as a joyous time.

I now see her aunt as another young Anne; the Lister women full of energy and intellect and a desire to travel, excepting Marian perhaps who seems denied these traits. Perhaps Anne stole her share? Her uncle never involved her aunt in the estate, though I'm sure she would have been perfectly capable. He did allow Anne involvement though, and her aunt tells me that was her doing in order to keep young Anne occupied. She needed a vocation and as most of them were barred to her because of her sex, why not allow her to be a landowner, the one thing not denied to her? By the time her uncle died, Anne knew what she was doing and could take over seamlessly. It sounds as if she has proven herself more capable than most of the male Listers before her, but I will not tell her that. It will go to her head.

Marian and I continue to grow closer and share more. She has become my substitute sister and I tell her about Elizabeth and her situation. I realise it sounds as if I am warning Marian away from marriage; I had quite forgotten her own courting! I assure her I only want to share as it's a burden on me, selfish really. I say that I'm sure her chap will be of a good sort, but the way Marian looks at me suggests she is not sure herself.

Marian's suitor comes over for supper with us and their father interviews him as he would a potential new Army recruit. The suitor stands his ground well at first, surrounded by our eclectic mix of four women and an ex-Captain, but begins to falter when asked what money he has and his political leanings.

Unfortunately, he shows some sympathy for the Whigs and all of the present company other than myself sigh in unison and the room falls silent. Poor fellow. So close, but he should have done his homework. I thought everyone knew the Lister's Tory politics. Obviously, Marian had failed to prepare him with answers beforehand, or did she know that this may be his undoing and allow him to walk straight into the trap? I cannot tell. Marian's face never gives much away. Other than Aunt Anne, the Listers have a knack of hiding their thoughts well with new people – a skill I should probably try to learn more of – and so I am left unsure of what they could possibly be thinking. Nevertheless, Marian does not mention him again and I have already forgotten his name.

Miss Lister

I'm thinking that this could be perfect. Our lives fall together, and it turns out she does have some business acumen. The more she learns from my running of Shibden, the more she takes stock of her own estates and incomes. She visits her collieries now too, and we are seen about town. She joins us in the Lister pew with my sister, aunt and father. Let others stare if they will, for what are we but four single women in each other's company? Surely, they must all see that it makes sense, all of us probably too old to marry and happy to remain spinsters. Why should we suffer loneliness because of it?

The world around us changes quickly and Halifax seems to prosper. The Walkers and their kin cannot help but be ever more successful. Ann struggles to spend her money, so I gladly oblige to help her. We shop together and treat ourselves, replacing all the curtains and bedding; we order the new dinner service we wanted from York and she agrees to all my plans for Shibden. The work is set in motion; a small piece at a time so as not to annoy my aunt or father with too many workmen at once.

My father, aunt and sister are all finally in agreement about knocking out the ceiling in the main hall and raising it to the full height of the roof. We will only lose one room upstairs for it, and the new staircase will be grand. I show them the drawings and I do not think they even mind me adding the initials A. L. into the woodwork. I later realise that the initials are also now my wife's and so in a way we are all three – my Aunt Anne, myself and my wife – immortalised in the woodwork with the Latin words *Justus Propositi Tenax* inscribed between them; our Lister motto, 'Just and true of purpose'. I order some finely turned posts for the stairs before they can change their minds, and add wooden figures for each of the banisters, including a lion clutching a shield with the Lister family crest. I shall make this a grand house yet.

I bring out of storage some portraits of our ancestors and have them repaired and reframed, so that we can adorn the new high walls with our family heritage when they are complete. I commission a local painter to capture Aunt, which she delights in, whilst Marian and Father both refuse to sit for portraits. Instead, I commission a landscape of Shibden for Marian and I leave my father to his newspaper which he reads as if he will be tested on it later and achieve a degree for the astute reading of it. He tuts and shares with us the parts that pique his interest as if he wrote the news or caused it himself.

One day I'll commission portraits of myself and Ann. I'm not sure if I'd like to have myself looking down from the walls just yet, as if I have already died. I worry that they'll never capture my likeness.

Miss Walker

The concern that we should do more for others plays on my mind. Sitting with Anne looking at our accounts, the two of us combined have monies to spare but she is intent on sacrificing more land to her 'landscaping' and building a lake which will serve no purpose but to add to her own grandeur. I tell her she has no one to impress as she has already won herself a wife, but she ignores me, and I know she'll go ahead with her plans regardless.

We argue over philanthropy. I want to contribute to the children's homes, but she would rather invest in a new museum of relics. She asks what the point in saving children's lives is if there is no heritage or culture to educate or interest them? Let them all suffer and die then, I say, as long as you have some art works for the elite to look at, then never you mind.

I always knew we would quarrel on some points.

Anne does not seem to have the same compassion that I do. She does not seem to notice the poor in the streets. As she strides along to buy fabrics and books, she does not even glance at the woman with a baby that cries with hunger, whilst I pass her a few small coins and feel my eyes burn with tears. I suppose she does not have the guilt that I bear: the Walker success came from industry, from the blood and sweat of others. Being primarily funded by rents, the Listers give people work and income and their tenants live well. Anne is kind to them. Even when they do not use their vote for her party, the Tories, she visits with cheese and honey and always tries to help if illness befalls them and they can no longer manage their stead. She threatens to cast them out if they do not agree with her politics or fall behind on rent, but she never does. She compromises privately, but in public maintains her fearsomeness; I imagine it is to make sure they do not take liberties and so she retains their respect, and a bit of fear for good measure. I admire how she does that, but cannot match it myself. However, now that I am aligned to Miss Lister, the men who work for the Walkers do seem to pay more respect to me. When I appear at the collieries with her by my side, I see how they eye us, fear us and wonder at us. I feel braver now than I have ever done, but we do argue.

Mr Lister, always so pleasant to me, calls me to the study one day and I quickly fill with fear that it has all been an act and now he will tell me to leave because he has realised what we get up to. I attend on him and he greets me with a smile. He tells me he has heard that there is a new orphanage to be built and takes my hand. He tells me I am a kind, sweet soul; however, the report of the orphanage clearly states thanks for a bequest from Miss Walker of Crow Nest in the newspaper. He pulls out the page, lets me read it and then casts it on the fire so that Anne will not see it. When she notices the page is missing later, he tells her an extravagant tale of a wasp in the room and him squashing it with the paper before disposing of the dirtied pages. It is too cold now for wasps, but Anne is barely listening as something else has caught her eye. He winks at me.

Her aunt and Marian, it transpires later, both read it too and so we are all in on it except Anne. I am delighted to be included and this small, inconsequential conspiracy makes me feel more accepted than any previous occurrence. We now have a secret, the four of us against Anne. I quite like it. Though incomparable to the secret of Anne and I, of course.

I wonder often if they know? If they would not care, or if they would cast us out if they discovered it? Luckily, we still have the Moss House to retreat to and it is in there, rather than in our rooms, that I feel most unbridled and free.

Miss Lister

If she agreed with everything I say, then she would become a bore. We read in the newspaper of improvements to working conditions and increasing the minimum age of children to work in the mills. Ann seems to want to rescue the lot of them. I know she gave handsomely to a new orphanage but I do not tell her that I know. My family think that they protect her from my scorn, but let them have their small allegiance to her; it does them all good. I would not have said anything anyway. They believe me to be far more of a tyrant than I am, and I must keep up the impression of it, so I do not say a word. I'm glad the Lister money does not come from industry, the toil of others. My conscience is clearer than Ann's, so let her contribute what she must to ease her guilt.

We trip to York more regularly now, sometimes with Marian in tow as well, and she joins me in visiting friends there, including the Bests and the Norcliffes. They seem to like her, and she grows ever more in confidence.

We take the walk into Halifax together and visit Whitley's, the local book seller and stationer where I order more books for my diaries; hardbound with good quality unlined paper. My order has arrived of Rosamund Best's publication of her paintings of all twenty-four churches in York. It's a surprise gift for Ann and she opens the package and turns straight to the page of Holy Trinity before we've even left the shop. We smile at each other at our secret union and walk home arm in arm.

Whilst some aspects of Halifax are on the rise, the town centre reveals the changes are not all for the better. The extravagant cloth hall, once a hub of activity on the Saturday of trading, is now beginning to decline. It will no doubt become just another common place for a market and fall to ruin. The wealthy pass in their ornate carriages whilst we cannot help but see the poor and starving all around us. I cannot bear to look at them and keep my gaze fixed on our purpose, but Ann suffers on behalf of each and every one she sees and sometimes I wonder if I should leave her at home to protect her from all this – but isn't this life itself? We cannot live in the delusion that everyone is as happy and content as our little family is at Shibden, with want of nothing but warmer weather.

Ann still seems in awe of my hobby to write my diary and watches me of an evening. I read aloud sections to her. She likes to select an old volume at random and let it fall open on a page. Luckily, she cannot read my handwriting well, or the coded sections, so I can freely read her a sometimes-edited version. In truth, there is little left of me she does not know, I just spare her the details. We are almost caught up with each other on our histories and I settle into the security that there will be no more revelations to surprise me or unhinge this tranquillity of knowing each other so well and sharing almost everything.

We have settled in well to our lives here but there is something I want to share with her still. Paris.

Miss Walker

Just when I am finally accustomed to our cosy life at Shibden, she harks on about travelling to Paris. I agree – why should I not? It will be an adventure after all, but only six months into living together, into our 'marriage', and off she wants to go. I knew this would be how she is, I'd just hoped for a little longer to grow accustomed to this new life and for my family to realise that this is a long-term, lifelong decision. But I do not take as much persuasion now. I am hers and she will protect me. Our

Lister family will be waiting for us when we return. I will follow her anywhere. Well, at least as far as Paris.

Miss Lister

Just a short trip, I promise. Testing the waters. I can tell she is secretly excited as I make plans. She seems healthier than she has ever been, and I feel an urgency to get her overseas before anyone else dies out of the blue and she is undone once more.

She makes a nervous but welcome companion. This trip is much better than my last venture alone. I finally have her with me, on a ship, on foreign shores. Farther than she has ever been before. I never let go of her hand. One step at a time. I reassure her we can return home any day and she allows herself to ease into our voyage and relaxes as we walk the Parisian streets I am so familiar with. I share my other world with her, and I hope she feels free here like I do, away from Yorkshire. Away from the business of managing estates and finances, where I can forget I have any responsibility, except for my delicate companion whom I fill with breads and cakes, art and fresh air.

Miss Walker

Once she has me safely ensconced in Paris, I tell her that I am enjoying it which encourages her to suggest we go farther afield. She wants to go to Switzerland again, so that she may share it with me. She seems intent on reliving her travels and I ask her – will it not be dull for you to go again? – but she says I give her fresh eyes and she wants to see my reactions to the beautiful places she has seen. She last went to Switzerland seven years ago, and as she recounts her ascent of one of the highest mountains, for a moment I think she wants me to climb the thing as well. Luckily, she reads the concern on my face and assures me we will admire it from the valley below. She has an inkling to undertake another ascent but knows that it will be without me. I say I can manage on my own while she risks her life and she teases me and asks when my adventurous spirit died. I remind her in turn that we are now off to Switzerland on a boat, and before I met her I did not dare enter the woods by my house alone. I do not tell her I still fear this.

She must be patient with me; all of this is new, but it infects me. I am truly enjoying this adventure. I am away from all that ails me, the warmer climes do me good, her enthusiasm creeps into me and I feel that by her side I could go anywhere. I am also comforted to know that our beloved Shibden and my new family await us when we eventually return and that too gives me such comfort. I can enjoy my place here on foreign shores all the more knowing a home awaits me. The letters from her family come addressed to Miss Walker and Miss Lister and I love that I am included, they see us together, and care to ask after my health and happiness as well as Anne's.

Switzerland is as stunning as she promised, like the Pennines of home but on a grander, snow-capped scale. The clouds cover some of the peaks as if they are part of Heaven. I understand her wish to climb above the clouds but know I do not have the strength for it. She reads to me the diary she wrote when she was here last, and we retrace her steps in the towns and lower hillsides. In this new landscape, away from all we know, I am able to push all the questions and all that society expects to one side, and I see that how I feel about her is simple. I love her.

She shows me the travel notes she has written and tells me of her intentions to write them up into a book to be published one day. I encourage her and she lets me read them myself, unlike her diaries which I know she edits as she reads aloud to me. I buy her a gift of a new blank volume from a stationer we pass, with much confusion as I do not speak a word of the language. I present it to her for her travel writing and she promises that it will be our next project on our return to Shibden; together, we shall write up her notes, edit them and create a volume for publication. Now, seeing France and Switzerland for myself, I make some notes of my own that we can add; it will be a collaboration, she says. I realise I am rather committing myself to further travel, but so be it. To complete a book together, what an achievement!

We wonder if we would ever dare publish it under the names Mr and Mrs A. Lister. Only time will tell.

I write to my sister of what a wonderful time we are having and all the new sights I am seeing. This letter goes to her home where Sutherland will read it and I picture him pawing it with his large dirty hands, passing it to Elizabeth with disdain and some comment or other about me.

I write to Mrs Priestley and Miss Whitaker and tell them what joys I am having with Miss Lister who has opened my eyes to the world. I tell them our journey here has much improved my health. I tell them of Anne's plans for us to venture farther to the Pyrenees and of Anne's ascent of Mount Perdu several years ago that no woman before her had accomplished, and how she hopes to make another. I even suggest next time I will make the ascent of a mountain with her, though I know none of us will believe this.

I do not tell any of them of the looks we receive, the asking after our husbands. How do they let you travel unaccompanied, they ask us? They assume Anne is a widow because of her black

161

clothes and she does not correct them, despite calling herself Miss. I ask her if it wouldn't be easier to call herself Mrs Lister and have done with it, and I could be Mrs Fraser and wear black too and they can assume we are two wealthy widows with a desire to get away from the rest of our lives in mourning – but she'll have none of it. She introduces us as Miss Lister and Miss Walker, her companion, before I can say differently. Sometimes when she leaves me as I am too tired to venture out, I am left alone with someone who will talk to me, perhaps a kindly lady who speaks some English, I explain that we were both engaged and that our fiancés died, so we are almost like widows and sought company in our shared loss. They sympathise, pat my hand and pay for more tea. I like this fiction that people can understand and accept us for. I just want to be accepted. I like the sympathy, the connection, but Anne would hate it if she found out.

Miss Lister

We are outsiders to everyone else in the world because of something we cannot help: love. I had thought to love was just between two people, but as time passes, I realise our love alone is not enough. If we must hide, are seen as shameful by those who are supposed to love us too, our love is diminished, made to feel wrong when it should feel right. How can we not live openly? If I chose to marry a woman then why could it not have been in the eyes of God in a church, surrounded by our family and friends who would have been pleased for us and blessed our union and accepted us for who we are: two women who love each other? How can there be shame in that? We cause no one else any harm but are harmed ourselves by it. If only I could have been like the other women I fell for, most of them able to love either sex and so able to fall to normality, to conform. But that would be a lie, an endless torment, to deny myself who I am, and to what end? To make others feel more comfortable in my presence? To make everyone else feel that the supposed natural order is intact?

Not wanting to scare her from future travels, I keep to my word and return her safely home after just a few weeks. I have given her a taste of the possibilities for our future. But on our return journey, I realise that I too am looking forward to going home. I am not returning begrudgingly, but because we have had a good time and want to share it with our family. We want to complete all the plans we have talked of at Shibden, finish the extensions, see the new lake dug and filled next to our Moss House, create our own romantic walk through the estate.

Our future together looks promising and I feel like a newly married husband, returning after his honeymoon to take up residence as master of the house with his beautiful bride. For the first time in so many years, I am happier than I have ever been – even more on this journey home than when we left a few weeks before. Shibden pulls us back and welcomes us with open arms.

Chapter Sixteen

Summer, 1835: A reminder of Halifax and all its simplemindedness

Miss Lister

Men are all bastards. Though I feel as though I should be a man in form and for feeling how I do for women, I cannot imagine I would be of such poor character as to be so vindictive towards others as men are. They feel threatened by those who challenge their ideals and political leanings, yet instead of rising to the challenge or seeking a solution, they reject forthwith any negotiation for sheer stubborn-headedness. Is it greed that drives them? Or the inferiority of the size of their cocks? If so, why should they fear mine?

I know that the men of Halifax fear me now that I am aligned with Ann. Even with Shibden Hall and estate at my command, I had never posed much of a threat to their way of life. Only now they see that Miss Walker and Miss Lister have aligned and between us we may have enough influence to sway the election. They do not like that I hosted Tory party meetings here at Shibden and donated to their funds. I am denied the privilege of a vote because of my sex and yet my tenants rely on me for their very income, so of course they should vote as

I suggest! Why should I not encourage my tenants to support my politics? They do not like it when a woman influences men's decision and men's lives.

Despite my desires for a Tory candidate, I would now rather us be left alone. Men can be very nasty when they are threatened.

Miss Walker

I do not know how she stands it.

She looked at it. Then at me. Then led us off down the road as if it was nothing at all.

They had created an effigy of us both and set light to it. Our forms were hanging in the street in plain sight. On fire! And she walked away. I could barely hide my tears. Thank goodness I had Anne's arm to cling to, else I may have fallen in a faint.

How is she so strong? She marched us all the way back to Shibden, all the while talking of other matters as if she had not seen it. When we were finally safe inside, I could not help but sob, but she just sat me down, ordered tea and told me to pull myself together. What did it matter, she said? Men will be men. They do not like that we have influence over voters and are making our own money, and as they daren't speak to our faces they do something to provoke us. The only thing we can do is *not* be provoked. She spoke to me as a teacher to a small child, but still I cried. I had been shaken. No one has ever done anything as horrible as this to me before, nor aligned me so openly to Anne.

I suppose I knew this would come, that no one would allow two women to be left in peace together. Just one year on from moving permanently into Shibden and all is undone.

What rumours there were already! And now to burn effigies of us together; it unites us as one, even though surely everyone knows that Anne does all the talking when it comes to business and politics. I'm just the little wife, drawn into her husband's trials. Why couldn't they have burned an effigy of her alone? I imagine by including me too they are trying to hurt her even more. She'll probably be more determined than ever in her campaign to solicit more votes now. Oh, why cannot they just give her a vote? Then she'd stop all this nonsense!

I'm not sure what upsets me the most: the effigies, the violence of the fire, the way they hung there like real bodies, or that fact that she did not react. I long to see just one tear well up in her eye – something to show that she is hurt. But she hides it well. She is the husband protecting his wife, and I will always just be the wife. I will never be equal to Anne Lister.

Miss Lister

She had seemed so together, so much stronger of late since moving in with us at Shibden. My influence must have rubbed off on her. Being at Shibden, away from Crow Nest, her aunt and busy-body family, I had thought had done her good. I had seen her striding about with more confidence and we'd sit together in the Lister pew. We had walked through town with our heads held high and I started to believe that this was the way forward for us. We had accepted each other, and I'd hoped that this small town would let us be, but at this one small setback she seems unravelled. I wonder if all I have achieved with her will be lost?

All my small steps of reassurance, giving her confidence and sharing our worlds, our very marriage, have all been undone in an instant.

I wish I'd had nothing to do with this election. It had seemed just, when I am denied the vote and feel so strongly about who should lead our region to a better future, to lean on my tenants to vote my way. But if it means losing her, she whom I have grown to love and care for and look forward to spending my life with, I would never have been so vocal. Leave them to suffer at the hands of their vote. Let them learn the hard way that I was right. The Halifax crowd might wish me to lie down under the old gibbet blade so they can cut off my head, but the thought of being at Shibden without her again makes me wonder what there is to carry on for.

I'm astonished at how I feel. I never meant to let this woman infiltrate my life so much, but she has won us all over. My aunt, father and even Marian love her company and they can tell she has made me happier, though they know not what goes on behind closed doors. Now, we are all set to lose her, for the shock of this may return her to confinement at Crow Nest and the care of her aunt.

If this is it, I will pack my things and head to Russia next week. Burning our effigies indeed!

As I thought. All men are bastards.

Miss Walker

We are daughters to fathers and sisters to brothers. We are passed from our father's hands to those of another man to whom we must answer and for whom we must provide sons, whom we will then be at the mercy of for all our lives. Men teach us, doctor us, pray for us, make laws which affect us and determine our fate. We never break out of the hands of men until we die. Why cannot they just leave us alone?

Mr Lister didn't manage to hide it in time. He couldn't help but start at it when he read it. We gathered to see what it was he'd seen and he tried to close the paper but Anne snatched it from him, gasped and threw it down. I picked it up, foolishly, and I too had the shock of my life to see it.

An announcement in the paper.

Once we'd all had a look, Marian left the room, always one to avoid Anne's temper. Aunt ordered more tea and busied herself with her sewing. I sat and cried, and Mr Lister ranted about small-minded folk, sounding much like Anne, who herself paced back and forth and then with a flourish threw the entire paper on the fire. Mr Lister had only read a few pages, but he showed his allegiance to Anne well enough by not commenting and then taking her out for a long walk around the grounds. I admire him more and more.

The announcement was for the wedding of Sir Jack Lister of Shibden Hall and Miss Walker of Crow Nest on election day. It was a slight against us both and our families.

No one but us two know of the wedding that really took place. I wonder if they could imagine the irony of it, that she is in fact wed to me. I wonder if they knew that it was true or if they simply meant it as an insult, that neither of us are now worthy of marriage to anyone but each other. If only we could be really married, legally! Perhaps we should put in a real announcement – but if we cannot even tell our own families, what chance do we stand? The businessmen we have riled and any opposition to her party will come and burn down the Hall with us all inside if they should find out.

A few weeks then passed, and I had hoped it was all over. Bullying, as Mr Lister had termed it. It was bullying, plain and simple. The lowest of the low. It comes from a place of jealousy and inferiority, he had stated loudly on more than one occasion.

He'd explained to me that those men see her, and me too, as a threat to their power and so resort to name calling, by which he meant the name Gentleman Jack, a name given to Anne years back when she first started to manage her own estate and sink her own coal pits, which has now resurfaced.

The situation seems to have worsened after the effigies. As we walk in town or attend church, men nod their heads and say, 'Sir, Miss,' to us, or call from afar: look who it is, Gentleman Jack! We do not recount this to the family of course; Anne never wants them to be concerned with it. But to publish in the newspaper, knowing everyone will read it, seems beyond cruel. We have received letters too, full of insults, one of them even offering to rescue me from the Listers. We try to laugh at them and ignore them. They are just words.

If only it had just remained as name calling.

But Anne comes home bloodied and will not tell us what happened. At night, once the candle is out, I feel her sobbing and hold her in my arms. It takes a lot for Anne to cry. I do not ask her about it, I just hold her and cry too, for when she hurts, I hurt. What they do to her, they do to me too; we are one in this. I am as angry as she is. Having now physically hurt her, I become afraid. What will they stop at?

Miss Lister

My father dabs the gash on my head with some stinging ointment and reassures me I will be all right, as if I am one of his men in battle. He does not seem to know what to say and I do not say a word. I wish I'd been out on a horse and could simply say I had fallen, but one does not just fall over when walking; not unless someone comes at you with a stick.

Father gets me drunk on brandy and I finally calm as the anger is drowned out by a numbness induced by the alcohol, which I rarely touch under normal circumstances. He holds my hand, an oddity for him, but I do not pull away. I do not call him a sentimental fool or ask him what he wants; he's holding my hand because he cares for me and so I let him. I do not want him to let go. I am a young girl again who has fallen from my horse and am trying to be brave so that he will continue to let me ride, but inside all I want to do is cry.

I had let myself feel immortal. I believed that it was just name calling, that the effigies and the letters meant nothing, that they would never dream of really hurting me. The assault is a reminder of my sex, my size, my weakness. At least they could have sent someone my own size so I had a fair fight, but no, he was a giant of a man. I tried to push him away, but he caught me with his stick which sent me to the ground like a struck skittle. I curled up tight thinking he would come again and rain down blows on me and, as I feared for a moment, end my life. But he did not. Fortunately, he just wanted to scare me and left me cowering in the dirt until I regained my senses and staggered home.

I did not want the others to see, but I could not hide the blood pouring down my face and onto my clothes. I was shaken and half senseless and fell into my father's arms. How weak of me; I am embarrassed.

How do I react to this, how do I move on? Now afraid to walk on my own land. Afraid to go outside. They want me to be afraid, to be a recluse, to hide away.

It is a reminder that what I reassure Ann and Marian, that we are safe, is a lie. We like to think that our place in society protects us, but the truth of it is we should all be afraid of them, of men, all of the time, as the only way to keep ourselves safe is to remain on our guard. I had let my guard down.

I shall have to carry a loaded pistol from now on. Damn them. Damn them all, is what I think. But I know not how I can win this.

Father sent an angry letter on my behalf to the newspaper for printing the wedding announcement, as the editors surely knew it would offend the Listers, long-standing supporters of the paper. He told them they should have checked with him first and should do so in future before printing any matters pertaining to the Listers. I let him write on my behalf. They replied with an apology. Now he wants to report the assault, but I beg him not to. It would not do any good. I never saw the man's face anyway. He could have been anyone.

He is angry for me, but he can never understand what it's like to be a woman. That we live with the constant fear that half the population is stronger than us and can overpower us at any time, without the slightest provocation. We women are the lion tamers, aware that our safety is an illusion, that the wildness can creep in any moment and the lion will remember his strength.

The next Sunday we all go to church in the carriage together. My father, my aunt, my sister and my wife. I let Father assert his protectiveness over the Lister clan as he escorts us into the church, leading his Lister women and our adopted Ann into his pew. He stands taller than I have ever seen him and looks quite fearsome as the folks around us stare on at the Captain who served his country. He is the Lister lion and we are his pride, following behind him, protected. Let them see the redness and bruising they have caused me.

Hidden from view behind the wooden pew, he squeezes my hand and whispers that he is proud of me. I have to hide my face in the hymn book, as it's all too much to be required to be so brave all the time, for all of them, and for Ann, when one has been reminded so brutally that it is all just an act; that anyone bigger than me can dash away at me with a stick.

I wonder if the culprit is sitting in the church, watching. I wonder if he'll be sent again to finish the job. I wonder about all the things he could have done to me.

I remember a time when the name didn't hurt me and I wanted to claim it as my own, but now it saddens me to my core. I do not wish to be Gentleman Jack. I hate the sound of it and all it encompasses. They have won. I will have nothing more to do with politics.

Miss Walker

Winter is upon us and whoever it was that had set against our quiet peaceful family with no malice towards anyone, will not let it end. Not even with the shedding of Anne's blood.

Not content with burning our effigies, insulting us in the newspaper, anonymous letters, even striking Anne, we are called out one night by the groom and race after him to see the flames tearing apart our Moss House. We stand helpless, the family, the servants, for what else can we do but watch it burn? There is no reason for it to burn other than malice. We all know, but do not speak it; this was no accident.

Our joyous little sanctuary goes up in smoke into the night sky. Everything we had created, enjoyed and loved, our little heaven, our haven, our home, becomes reduced to ashes. We had been in there only that morning.

The heat of the blaze warms us against the cold winter air that surrounds us as we stand there; a line of Listers silhouetted against the bright flames in the dark night.

After a while, without words, Mr Lister leads Aunt and Marian and the others back up to the Hall. I remain with Anne. I never wish to leave her side. I hold her hand as she stands, motionless, watching the flames. I do not know what she is thinking but I fear its outcome.

It takes some hours to burn and my back aches and my feet freeze but I will not leave her. I too want to see it end, every last piece of it destroyed, the full extent of someone's cruelty towards her, us, all of us.

In these hours, my mind races with questions. What if it had been Shibden itself? What if we'd been inside? Do they know what went on here, is that what this is about? What do they want from us? To withdraw entirely from life? To leave here? To die? Or is this the end of it? The final attack? Will we give them what they want? Close our doors to outsiders? Live out our days here and care not what happens outside our walls? Forgo our places in church, our familiar streets and haunts, our trips to York, give up the carriage, put high walls around our house?

But in time, as I stand and watch our Moss House burn, my mind quietens, and the flames become beautiful and I am lost instead to the idea of the two of us, standing here, our faces hot from the fire and our backs cold against the winter night, paying our respects to our own little chapel of sorts. I fall calm and wonder what our lives will bring next.

In the days that follow I worry that I may lose her; that some part of her may close to us. She defends herself from these attacks by not reacting, but in doing so removes herself from us too. She buries her pain deep inside and never speaks another word of the Moss House. I wonder if she is defeated and this is her acceptance, or whether she is biding her time, coming up with a plan. Is she plotting her revenge? It she planning a war?

Chapter Seventeen

Spring, 1836: The ruin of the Moss House and departures from Shibden

Miss Lister

Snow fell on the remains of the Moss House and for a for a short while made the ugly pile disappear; but after the snow thawed, I had not the strength to rebuild it and now simply avoid going near it altogether.

Winter has passed, and we have been left alone for some time now. Life ticks on at Shibden with our daily routine that protects us and keeps us together like the cogs in a clock, keeping time and order with an occasional chime.

With all the stresses on our family last year, I imagined I'd lose Aunt first. But the winter was harsh and even though the days grew longer and some warmth returned, Father seemed to have lost all his strength. Of all the days to die he chose my birthday, tarnishing the day for the rest of my life. It was warm that morning, warm enough to go for a long walk with Marian after his body had been taken away.

He died in the night. I found him in his bed in the morning, looking surprised, a present for me wrapped next to his bed. I opened it to find a beautiful compass with a note: 'For Anne, so you can always find your way home'.

Perhaps it was not Shibden that was my anchor but Father. His presence since my birth, unfaltering, a devotion to me, of sorts, always on my side. His generous soul that let us all find our own path, never judging, never questioning.

Marian seems unable to cope. She clings to Aunt and to Ann; I am left to watch on as the women mourn and I keep my own tears to myself. I now step into the breach and must remain strong for them. I am in charge.

It is all left to me now, excepting my aunt's share. There are no more Lister men.

I am closer to what I wanted when I was young, to be the sole heir, the owner outright, the decision maker; but having it now feels hollow. If the last few years here had been different, perhaps I would feel more satisfied. If I had felt part of my class, accepted as a fellow landowner and businessman, if I'd been on committees as I should have been and not barred because of my sex, perhaps...

Now I have no place in society. They will not let me in. Even now, taking Father's place as the official head of our estate, there is no place for me. They keep me locked out, as if I am a plague that will infect them all.

Ann assumes I am all confidence, but she does not see what it takes to stand in a room full of men. To ignore the jibes, the eyes on you, knowing that if they should decide, any one of them could snap my neck and have done and they would not be accountable for it, because they are the law, and any power we women have is merely in the hope that they respect us enough not to hurt us, or that they do not realise how fragile and weak we are.

As I walk beside his coffin to our Lister corner of the church with my three charges following sadly behind me, the responsibility for them bears down on me and I worry that I cannot protect them from anyone who may try to take away our freedoms. Anyone who may insult us. Anyone who may wish to damage our property like they did the Moss House. Anyone who may try to strike them.

Aunt is frail and Marian seems older, more gaunt, past any chance of a match now, beholden to me entirely. My Ann, so beautiful still, but carrying the weight of the world on her gentle shoulders. Eyes are on her throughout the service; they cannot look away as she weeps for Father. They cannot understand the grief of this wayward Walker; who was he to her, they question? When, if life was fair, he would have been her father-in-law and they would sympathise.

Even familiar faces, the Priestleys, the Norcliffes, Mariana and old Lawton, who have all journeyed over for the service, look upon us as a sorrowful sight. All four of us now dressed in black, like a Lister uniform. I look around the church and note how they have all dressed like me for this saddest of occasions. I no longer stand out; all of us are joined together on this one day where my colour is everyone's.

He is lowered into the ground, watched and mourned by his two single daughters, his single sister, and a single stray who was swept into his home and fell under the Lister curse: to be an outsider.

None of us knows what to say. People whom I have known my entire lifetime give me their condolences, but do not look me in the eye.

How brave of Father to have accepted us as we are, to have created a home for us and taken us all in. I shall miss him terribly.

Miss Walker

To try to stop myself from crying in the church, I busy myself looking at Mariana and Isabella, the women who have had orgasms with my wife. It should have been just us four left alone to grieve, but funerals are a spectacle, an event; even military folks turned up, all uniforms and medals, people we'd never seen before who pledged they knew Mr Lister well, and there she stood, having to smile and thank each one of them, hear their condolences. She is so brave, my love. I later sit with Aunt who also seems so frail now, the last of her generation, as the sisters go out for a walk after the funeral.

No sooner is Mr Lister buried than pother starts up again. Even in our grief, after we believe all the election nonsense is over and done with, someone poisons our well and then our coal mines are sabotaged. We are defenceless and can do nothing to stop them or retaliate. We let our stewards fight our corner and clear up the damage on our behalf. We do not go to see for ourselves, but hide away in Shibden as they want us to. Will they never leave us alone?

Marian confides in me that she is glad she is the youngest and does not have to deal with all this. She is happy she has Anne, and I squeeze her hand and tell her I am glad we both have her.

Aunt soon takes to her bed and does not seem to improve. Doctors come and go with little to offer. Marian sits with her for hours and hours and says she will not lose her too, but all our will and prayers cannot save her.

Miss Lister

As the temperature drops and the days shorten, my aunt breathes heavily. I send Marian away to get some rest. She kisses her and clings to her and then drags herself away.

Summoning her remaining strength, my aunt tells me that I am braver than she was, and I laugh. She tells me how pleased she was that Marian and I came to live with them, that we gave her and my uncle a new life. She grips my hands and tells me to look after Marian and I promise I will try. Then she lectures me that I should make sure I am surrounded by family, that being alone is no good for me, and neither is being with just one person, by which she means little Ann. It is other people, friends, family, she says, that make us who we are. Put that in your diary so you do not forget it, she tells me.

Only a few days after this and the three of us sit around her after the doctor has left with a sorrowful shrug. We watch on helplessly as she lies there, barely aware of us, our hands holding tightly onto hers, as she struggles to breathe and in a moment we all witness, stops. She falls still, as though something has left her body and all that is left is a vessel, an empty corpse. I think of the spark of new electricity that could revive her. Whatever it was that had given her form life, been our aunt, has gone and does not linger.

I try to write in my diary seeking solace in the words, but they are splashed with tears which flow as my words dry up.

As my aunt joins her brothers in Heaven, I wonder what they think when they look down at us three that are left, pacing the house, none of us speaking, breathing in the cold air which tastes of melancholy.

Shibden Hall now finds itself inhabited by three orphans, all of us in black.

Miss Walker

I notice at the funerals that Anne is no longer separate from us as we are all of us in black, all as one – yet Anne's head remains high, her face fixed. Anne, I realise, will never blend in. Perhaps she should have worn red, or white.

I do not know how she manages it when my entire body shakes with tears and I cannot stop their flow. I can see them watching me, judging me, for who am I to sit with the Lister family? Both times I should have gone to my own pew and sat with my own aunt and the Priestleys, but when I say this to Anne she simply says, sit wherever you want to sit. I choose her. Once in the pew she holds my hand tight the whole time. Anne understands. My grief for her father and aunt is genuine, but she knows that my grief is not just over the death of these two; it is grief for all of them gone before which overflows. My tears may seem excessive to some, but Anne knows why they fall so readily. She told me later she could not help but think of her brother Samuel too, and in these long cold winter nights we hold each other and cry freely, away from the public show, away even from Marian as Anne does not wish her to see her upset. She tells me that in other countries they mourn more openly; they throw themselves on the coffin and wail and shout and scream and cry. What a release, she said, to be able to let it out. Whilst we English are expected to keep it inside and so carry it with us for the rest of our days. I agree, but think that I cry all the time and it never seems to lessen. I do not tell her this, and ponder what would be a release for me? I think perhaps if we could receive something like a medal for each loss, to wear with pride, and show others what we have suffered, lived through, endured. Let them see our sorrow borne upon our breast and give us pity and understanding.

I think of my parents, my brother, friends, aunts, uncles, the fiancé I knew so fleetingly, all snatched from us, and fall to mourning for all that has passed and all that cannot be. The questions rise up in me: where are they now, are they looking down on us, do they see me here in her arms, do they judge me, is that why I must lose them all, is this punishment for what I have chosen to feel and chosen to love?

The spiral begins again, and I hold Anne tight in the hope that she will not let me fall far. This time, though, she has her own grief and I cannot allow myself to fall into mine when she needs me. We need each other now more than ever.

Miss Lister

There is space in the Lister corner of the church for me. Me *and* Marian. Are we the last two? The space will be full then. The end of the Listers, as if the place assigned for our coffins knew before we did, that we would be the end of the line. There are some cousins in Wales and America, but what would they care of little Shibden? Although much improved by my additions, there is so much work still to be done. But I have the rest of my life for that. Right now, while I am still healthy and have a companion to take with me, the world awaits.

I look around at the weekly congregation and no longer see the faces of friends. They are just people whose lives once crossed with my own. Do any of them care for Miss Lister, Miss Walker and Shibden? Would any of them wonder where we went if we were to disappear? Would any of them anticipate our return? Perhaps it is my own fault for not being as great a philanthropist as others in the region. I never felt I had spare income for that, but perhaps that is what would have made the faces kinder to me. Shutting myself away at Shibden, remaining within the same narrow circle of friends may have kept me from my people. I delved into Halifax politics and the Literary and Philosophical society but never felt welcome in either.

I like to think I have cared for my friends and tenants and helped where I could, but I never felt as though I was from Halifax, just from Shibden. I am Anne Lister of Shibden Hall. It is its own small island in Yorkshire of which I am now solely in charge. From when I first moved in with my aunt and uncle, it was Shibden I loved. Although I would leave it, I would always call it home, miss it, return to it and seek to improve it.

The thought keeps coming to me that there is nothing here for me now. Marian threatens to leave us and go back to Market Weighton, but she does not, she is tied to Ann. Even the changes to the Hall have little interest for me now. It feels empty. Ann finds no pleasures here. I wonder why we stay. Perhaps the time is now to leave this place, these people who have vexed us, and once more venture out into the world, but this time I travel safe in the knowledge of what awaits me on my return; my home. My new library will be waiting for me, and with Ann's money and mine we can ever improve it and live in peace, the two of us; but peace is far from my mind at the moment. In another five or ten years perhaps, but now the world awaits.

It's just a shame that my beloved has the enthusiasm of a snail. Never mind, I shall drag her with me and rest assured when she sees the oceans, the mountains, she will fall in love with the world as I have, and we will both want to see and walk over as much of it as we can, while we can.

Although I do not like to admit it, if I do travel, this journey may well be the last. When I return to the completed Shibden, my tower library waiting for me, this time I may not be lured away again, but reside the rest of my days at the Hall, writing up my travels to share with others, overseeing the final building works. I suppose I could then share some of the Lister income with those less fortunate than I. But they'll have to wait. I must enjoy myself first.

Whilst I am deeply saddened to lose Aunt, Ann and Marian mope about together, feeding off each other's grief. Marian declares that if we are leaving her to travel then she does not wish to be left here at Shibden alone. Then come with us, I say, and she refuses. I have never been able to fathom what goes on in her mind.

Miss Walker

As Anne and Marian's voices rise ever higher to best each other and be heard, though we are all in close proximity, Marian tells me I could stay here with her instead, and let Anne go off travelling by herself, and for the briefest of moments I rather like the idea. Perhaps Anne reads it on my face, as she is suddenly struck with a jealousy I have never seen before, and instead of leaving me behind with Marian, she decides to rid us both of her, our sister and dear friend, by declaring loud enough for the whole of Halifax to hear:

She's my WIFE! She will come with ME!

And there you have it. I suppose it had to come out eventually.

We watch poor Marian's face as she realises the full extent of our relationship and does not know where to look.

She packs her bags and returns to Market Weighton once and for all, leaving us both.

Chapter Eighteen

1837 – 1838: Two orphans in black

Miss Lister

As I survey the home that will pass through our family and see the world change when we are all dead and buried, I realise that the lion carved on the staircase is Father holding our shield that bears the Lister crest. We have our initials engraved in the ceiling by the stairs, A. L. to represent all the Annes of Shibden, and there he is at the entrance to the stairs, keeping watch, proudly standing under our Lister motto.

I commission a large stone version of the same lion to stand next to the Hall, six feet tall, to greet guests or warn them off. It is a vicious lion, anthropomorphic in its form but a lion nonetheless, like the one I saw all those years ago in York at the mercy of the tamer, but this one is free, he chooses to stand there. The Lister lion is Father – or is it perhaps me, as I pick up the Lister shield and try to defend us?

Now so withdrawn from local life, I try to focus on our immediate surroundings, the landscaping completed with the waterfall and ponds, the apple trees planted and new kitchen gardens in use. The gatehouse nears completion and the lake is almost full.

Is it all just folly, I wonder? Do I spend our money just to amuse myself, give myself some control, some achievements? Or is it a reward for my work, for my loss? Is it a vent for my frustration at all I could have been if allowed: a scholar at the forefront of science, a collector, a Justice of the Peace or a Member of Parliament? I practise speeches I could give in my head, but when I speak out loud my voice reminds me of what I am.

I continue to study and make notes and lists of questions that will never be answered; there is so much more to discover and the world moves on without any influence from little me. Hidden away here in my half-formed castle, what impact can I make? No one calls upon us now. We are forgotten.

My diary pages still fill. I cannot give it up; even on my darkest days I still must write. It is my addiction, but what will come of it? What will become of the volumes all neatly lined up on my shelves behind the panelling? What will become of us?

Ann will not come with me into Halifax to hear the proclamation, which serves also as the first carriage drive down our newly built road and past the nearly finished gatehouse. She sulks and remains inside as she has for much of the last year since Marian left. I fear to leave her alone with just servants for company, but I cannot miss this.

I tell her it would mean a lot to me and she can stay in the carriage, but she worries there will be large crowds. I give up, storm off by myself and take the maids with me instead who are excited by the prospect and quickly don their best bonnets and shawls.

We travel down my new road and past the gatehouse, to be completed any day now, and we turn left onto the main road towards Halifax to join the flow of traffic into town. An air of celebration greets us as the traffic slows to a halt and families get out and walk, leaving their carriages behind. I see the Priestleys and they beckon me and my maids over as if we are old friends, and we walk with them into the town centre. The throng of the crowds excites me. Once caught up in the noise, the bodies pressed close together, I am just one of many; no one looks at me, I am lost in amongst the hundreds, thousands even that have gathered. I feel alive again as we hear the announcement: Queen Victoria has been crowned as our new sovereign. The crowd cheers and chants God Save the Queen over and over, and strangers shake hands and pat each other on the back as if we have all jointly achieved something, and for those few hours, I am a part of society again. I do not want to go back to Shibden, at least not for a while.

I give the groom and the maids a coin each and the rest of the day off. I travel back with the Priestleys and spend the afternoon with them, like old times, with no mention of why we have not spoken but for pleasantries for three years. It is as if Mrs Priestley and I are agreeing to forget, and of course Mr Priestley knows nothing. I can tell.

We talk about our female sovereign and what changes she may make. I wonder what this may mean for the rest of us women, to be led by a woman again after more than a century; will she raise us up too, or does she not really have any power either? Perhaps she does not care. I do not speak of this with the Priestleys, who would not entertain such nonsense as discussing women's futures.

That night, with Ann asleep in my arms, I silently pray to the new Queen to realise that if she can rule the country as a woman, she could also allow others at least some chance of education, a chance to be listened to, a chance to vote without judgement.

I ask Ann to join me on a trip into Halifax again. She refuses, but I'll not miss the laying of the foundation stone on my own bloody building. I shall not roll over and die just yet. Northgate House, which had sat idly by for years, has finally been renovated into a hotel, and now we will start works on an adjoining building with a spacious saloon for dancing and parties: a casino. Our new joint Lister-Walker venture. I want to leave my mark on Halifax, and if nothing else it has been a project to occupy me. I'll make it a success, then I'll rent the thing out and never have to venture into town again, with or without her.

To my surprise, Ann eventually agrees to come and even offers to say some words herself at the ceremony. She wants us to appear as partners in the endeavour, to show all her cousins, who will no doubt be in attendance, that she is not some meek companion but is making her own decision to invest. I admire her for suggesting this and encourage her.

Now, though, sat in the carriage as we turn out onto the main road into Halifax, she quakes next to me at the thought of public speaking, but I will not let her back out of it. It will do her good, and for them to see her. The last time many folks saw us together was at Aunt's funeral, and now here we are in triumph. Let them stare, let them judge! At least they'll see that she's alive and I've not drowned her in the lake and kept her money.

As we approach the hotel, over a hundred people have gathered and I wonder if they are here for the spectacle of the new building or the spectacle of us.

We bury some coins and an inscription placed inside a green glass bottle. We make our speeches and receive applause. For a moment, I could forget our troubles and feel somewhat part of the town and its people once more. Has enough time passed for us to make more of ourselves again? Then I remember the pistol tucked underneath the seat in the carriage and that I had asked all my men to attend, and here they stand around us like guards, as if we were royalty perhaps. I eye the crowd to see if I can discern a tall broad man carrying a stick, willing to bludgeon someone, even a woman, for a fee and the spite of another.

Miss Walker

I say a few words and thank God when it is over.

Anyone would think she owned the town. She does not notice how they look at us. She seems to have forgotten all that has been done to her, to us. Our beloved Moss House that someone burned down and for which the culprit was never found.

It takes eight men to lower the large stone down into the spot, like the lowering of a coffin into a grave and I feel rather flattened that perhaps the bottle will be crushed under the weight of it and will not survive to be found in the future. Who would ever lift this stone again anyway, I wonder? Would they care for a note and coins left by two women as if it were somehow important?

Anne then speaks about her hometown and her interest in its prosperity; she proclaims that the work on this new building should be a credit to us all. I can feel them squirm, those who have wronged us, spoken ill of us, and to ensure that she has made her point as I try to hide my blushes, she turns preacher as if she has been practising her speech, and says, may the voice of discord never be heard within the hotel's walls, may persons of every shade and varying opinion meet together here in amity and charity. They believe she talks of politics and business rivalries and the applause grows to cheering as if all is forgotten and forgiven on both sides. For a moment I believe it too. I look to the woman I love and love her even more for her words, her bravery, her defiance, and then I see a few men peel away from the back of the crowd, shaking their heads, and despite the loud cheers that follow us as we climb back into our carriage and the waves as we depart, it is the few men I think of; for although the whole seems friendly, supportive, it is the few that I fear. It only takes a few to spread rumours, to poison wells, to injure us, to burn down our Moss House.

Miss Lister

I manage to lease the hotel quickly and so it is out of my hands, the business all done with.

I am then invited to the laying of a foundation stone for a new museum by the Halifax Literary and Philosophical Society, of which I am a member. The only woman, of course. Ann refuses to come with me. Though I would like to attend and think it would be good for us to be seen together on more than one occasion, she tells me she did not enjoy the last event which rather dampens my spirits and crushes my memory of it as a pleasant occasion. We argue over it and she tells me to go alone but I do not wish to, not now that we have been seen together. We should continue in the same vein. I end up not going and stomp about the Hall.

I read in the newspaper the next week that there had been a photographer there. I should have liked to have been immortalised in a photograph. I should have liked us both to have been photographed together. It makes me think upon my own mortality. I am now forty-six years old. I must write some travel books; they will be my legacy. I wonder who will read them?

I could turn to my diaries for publication instead, but when I start to read them as an editor it all seems mundane, like a poor novel. I could publish them anonymously and edit my relationships so that they appear to be with men, transform it into a romance novel about a long-suffering heroine who simply cannot find the right man until one day she meets a neighbouring heir and they live happily ever after. No one would believe it, or care.

I conclude that I need to travel again in order to write a book to be published. Everyone has already been to Europe, so it must include somewhere that has been less written about. Russia calls me. I shall write 'A Woman's Journey Beyond the Continent.'

Miss Walker

She holds the atlas in front of me like a threat and makes me follow her finger as it darts across the edges of land masses and arrives on the ominous pages of Russia and other countries whose names I cannot pronounce.

With her family all gone and the Hall in progress, never expanding quickly enough for her to be satisfied, she wants to leave. Her answer is to run away. When I fear to even go a mile into Halifax, how does she think I can travel across the globe itself?

Miss Lister

Another year of our lives has passed as my atlas now gathers dust. Ann will hear no talk of travel and I concede to her. We remain hidden away here at Shibden and still she laments for all that was and can only look back, despite our lives together and all the potential for our future lying before her. She is only thirty-five but seems so much older; she acts as if her life is done with. She believes she never deserved the happiness we once had, as if it no longer stands before her, and I am left pleading with her to open her eyes and see me.

I even write to Mariana for advice, but she has none. What a pair we make, Mariana and I, both of us wedded and both of us trapped. If only Ann were twenty years my senior, like Lawton is to Mariana... what an awful thought.

I pace around my cage of Shibden, sometimes avoiding her altogether for an entire day, busying myself in the grounds, checking on the new lake and sitting in the new gatehouse with the doors locked so that I can be alone behind the castle walls I have created. I make it quite cosy in there and no one knows as they pass by on the busy road outside that the owner of Shibden Hall cowers inside. It is my new Moss House, this time built with stone walls and only I may enter.

How has my life come to this? I am more alone than I have ever been. Had I swallowed my pride and faced my own fear of being single I would now be free to leave, perhaps court someone new. The irony of it makes me laugh at my own situation; I am a husband trapped in a loveless marriage. Is that not what I dreamed of, to be wed? And here we are, like all other couples, wondering how we ever tolerated each other. I take pleasure by myself, imagining we are back in the Moss House together, but it is harder to concentrate, the pleasure takes time to rise in me. I allow myself to think of Mariana instead but that does not always help. My body is in league with my mind, both full of torment and unable to quieten, unable to find release. Sometimes the pleasure does not come to me. I circle and push against myself, become rough with myself. She has broken me.

Yes, I care for her and would not wish her ill, but my love for her lies in the memories of courting, our time in the Moss House, our wedding, our first travels to Paris... but then the storm clouds gathered and we lost those we loved and were shunned by our friends, family and society itself. I thought I could cope with the loss of everyone else if I had her. I thought she alone would be enough to complete me and fill my days, but Aunt was right. One person alone is not enough. We need people. And now it is as if she is no longer with me, as though I am abandoned by her too. I know she cannot help it, but how can she be so selfish and cruel as to shut me out? She forces me to hide in my gatehouse and listen to the traffic pass by for fear I should see someone who will ask me, as always, how is Miss Walker, and I must smile and say very well thank you, when it is all a lie, she is not very well at all. Neither am I.

I hope and pray that she can find her way through this and come back to me. I bring over Doctor Belcome from York but he leaves with a shrug. No one can help her. I will give her until summer to improve. Otherwise I shall have to run away, for any more of this loneliness will be too much for me to bear.

Miss Walker

As soon as we wake, I dread the day. I must somehow function and have the maids see me. I am anxious about what letters will come, what the newspaper will say, if someone should call on us, if someone should burn down the Hall with us both inside.

She reassures me all the time and protects me from the world. I know she checks the letters, reads the paper before me, meets people elsewhere so they do not come to the Hall. She has not told me, but I know she takes a pistol with her when she ventures out. She takes the carriage with the groom if she must go into town and goes straight to the bank or a shop and retreats again. She is no longer involved in the estate, it is all done through her steward who calls in each day to update her and receive orders. She goes out for her walks, but very early or very late in the day when the tenants will be at rest. She never goes out after dark and never mentions the hotel or visits it, never talks of any more plans for the estate except for the immediate plans for Shibden Hall itself. She only speaks of her library, currently being added to the Hall in the form of a tall tower, where she will be on the top floor, looking out, hidden up a spiral staircase. A library big enough for all her books and a desk, but not big enough for the two of us. It is her library alone; I do not seem to be invited. It is not mine, but probably comes from my money. I do not mind; she is looking after me, why should she not be rewarded with her own library for her precious books and writing her diary?

I finally agree to another trip for fear of losing her. But I only agree to France.

I arrive in Paris in a daydream. I let her take me. I play no part in it but do not refuse to go. I can no longer protest.

Familiar Paris again; it is four years since we were here. We walk the same streets and visit the same places and it feels like *déjà vu*, only this time we are quieter, our words do not flow, we are slower, more subdued. I write to Elizabeth but no one else. She whisks us on to Brussels where I have not been before and for a short while its novelty encourages us to talk more and enlivens me, but my back begins to ache once more and ever more often she leaves me in the rooms as she goes out without me. I am waited on alone in the hotel and served teapot after teapot; I sit and try to read the same book over and over, but I cannot fall into it, cannot be immersed. I am numb in a foreign town with ill-tasting tea that grows lukewarm before I finish a single cup.

I decide to write again to Marian, begging her to forgive us and to come save me from loneliness at Shibden when we return, for I cannot do this again. I cannot just sit and wait for Anne and then ride in a carriage for hours at a time and then sit and wait again like I am just some maid, growing ever more detached from the world, ever more detached from Anne. I must set her free.

France and Belgium do not quench her thirst and when I flippantly suggest she climbs another mountain, we are off into the Pyrenees where the cold air gives me aches and pains all over and I can never get warm. She leaves me in the care of strangers as she sets off to climb to a summit without me and I wonder if she will make it back to me alive, and how I would have to manage without her if she fell, escort her broken corpse back all those miles home to empty Shibden. If she should fall, she will take me with her – for how can I live on without her?

Miss Lister

It is over ten years since I made my last ascent to this height. This time I am the first person ever to do so. I convinced some local guides to take me where no one had been before. Reluctantly, and no doubt bemused by this English woman, who they no doubt thought would fail, they were swayed by the money I offered them.

Here I stand, triumphant. I am free. It is just me, in my body, away from the world, above everyone else living on it. I am at the summit of Vignemale. I make the first ever ascent on the seventh day in August 1838. I am the first to claim it, conquer it. I am forty-seven years old, and my body is more aware of my age than my mind is; it aches and my feet are raw. I'm too old for this climbing nonsense but would not give this up for the world. It has taken days to get here after bad weather delayed my guides and me on two attempts, but we persevered and slept under the stars and climbed in the dark to get here. Should I die here, right now, I would be content.

When on top of the world, the mind travels to the overriding vision of one's own existence, one's own life. I think of how much I have achieved and loved and lost. The rest of my life stretches out before me, but it is in tedium.

I had forgotten that my family was not immortal; I'd pictured us together at Shibden forever, but in truth we only had a few years together, the five of us. Then Father and Aunt were lost, and now Marian is gone from us. We have few friends left to visit, no new acquaintances. Mariana seems a distant memory; so few letters pass between us now. Didn't I tell her everything, once? I wish she were with me now.

I care for Ann, love her, but she no longer completes me. I am no longer whole. Was I ever?

Here I stand on the peak of a mountain no person has ever climbed before, and I am alive and happy, yes, but the experience will fade as soon as I take the first step back down. It will become just another memory, another experience recorded in my diary.

I will publish this account. This could be a travel article. But pessimism creeps in and I wonder who would read it. Others have made ascents, after all; it is not new. Would they even believe a woman capable?

Perhaps I am no longer permitted to enjoy life. Perhaps I have already had my allocation of happiness, and now I am given just contentment, no more. As I look out over the clouds which are now beneath us, hiding the world from our sight, I have a memory of my aunt and I in Paris, laughing, and a wave of grief washes over me as I realise that I cannot tell her of this. She will never know. I trudge back down three thousand feet and every single step feels like I am walking closer to nothing.

When we are reunited, I hold her close to me, my little Ann. I do love her, but we are cast from the world and a distance now stands between us that feels insurmountable. Ascending the mountain seemed easier than conquering her again.

Miss Walker

Travels completed, like a chore I must endure and feign happiness for. How awful that I cannot find the joy I once felt. I see it in her, and because I love her and do not want to lose her, I accompany her. I am weary to my bones when we return home and I sleep for days with the weight of it finally lifted.

Would it be easier to live a lie? To pretend otherwise? To find an old widower and beg him to take my hand? Or for each of us just to be alone? Yet in each other's arms we hold each other as if we will never let go. As if we are the only two people in the world. Many days I wish we were. Who is there truly that cares for me but Anne?

I wonder ever more why she stays with me and does not cast me back to Crow Nest. When I voice this, she kneels before me and promises me she loves me and will be with me forever. She tells me over and over that I am her wife and that she will never leave me and will do anything for me, but I see how much this plays on her; my silence, my tears that I cannot help but let fall. She is trapped here with me and she paces back and forth, back and forth, and for all her protestations that she will wait for me, care for me, never cast me out and never leave me, I see her as a lion. Trapped. One day someone will leave the door open and her wildness, so supressed inside her over all these years with me, will overcome her, and she will start to run and keep running and never look back. Anne is the Lister lion we pass each day on the carved staircase. Anne is the six-foot stone lion that stares at anyone who arrives or leaves Shibden. Who am I to keep her caged?

Miss Lister

Just the two of us for Christmas Day.

All those years I begrudged the presence of my family and now I miss them terribly. Marian did at least pay us a brief visit, but it was like meeting a stranger. She has gone the way of Mrs Priestley, cold and aloof, as if she has closed her doors to us. I hold her closely as she leaves; can she not see that I am her sister still, who cares for her and loves her? Why does she care what we do alone, in private? It does not change who I am or what I feel. I'm glad Aunt and Father did not live to see how we sisters turned out. We never got on well but we did love each other. Aunt told me to look after Marian, but she is lost to me.

I decide to try for some pleasure with Ann. It has been too long. I am kind and gentle to her all day and sneak a few kisses to her cheek as I pass her by and she smiles, and by the time we are seated for supper I squeeze her hand and run my fingers across her cheek and gently loosen one of her curls. I play with her feet under the table, even as we are served food, and she giggles. For a moment I am transformed to our earlier days, but she pulls her feet back out of reach. I persist and continue to catch her eye as I ask her about her plans for the coming year and top up her wine.

At night I hold her close to me and start to kiss her passionately on the mouth and she accepts. Perhaps this is my Christmas present. She allows the kisses but does not push into me, but I continue. I run my hand up her nightdress on the outside of her leg and pull her hips towards me; again she allows me.

We start to clutch at each other and kiss messily, grabbing at each other's mouths with lips and teeth and I think I have won her over. She allows me to remove her nightgown and I cast mine off and throw it high into the air with a flourish and she giggles again, that beautiful innocent ripple of noise I realise I have not heard for such a long time.

As our warm bodies and lips press together I finally feel free, content and, dare I say it, in love again. I pull back to look down into my lover's eyes and, hoping to see the same reflected back at me, I see instead the opposite. I realise that Ann has everything a woman could ever desire to be happy, except the very power to enjoy it, and there is nothing I can ever do to change that.

And instead of compassion and understanding, I am repulsed by this. How can she not let me in? Let me love her? Tease me so?

I have given her all my love but it is not enough. We are separate now and the isolation of it crashes down on me and I feel myself turn angry. I take hold of both her wrists in my hand and continue to kiss her all over her body and squeeze firmly her breasts, her thighs, I allow my weight to bear down on her and her face hardens as she starts to squirm and pull her hands free. I push against her harder and pinch her and push my fingers into her, but she pushes me away and I let go as I see a flash of fear in her eyes as if I am a stranger. I sit back on my heels, the connection between us lost. She lies there looking up at me, angry. How could I be so cruel? I have allowed myself to be angry at her. I soften and smile and kiss her mouth again gently and turn her away from me and hold her carefully in my arms as I caress her soft back, shoulders and arms and she lets me. I try to fix her with my hands. I whisper that I love her, but she does not reply to me.

It is New Year's Eve, 1838. Now it is I who cries, and Ann does not even turn to look at me.

Chapter Nineteen

1839: A departure from Shibden Hall

Miss Lister

Spring has come of a new year and the Hall's first stage of alterations is complete except for the windows in my tower. However, it has all taken too long and there have been so many frustrating setbacks; it has all felt too much. My grand plans for more works will have to wait. If it takes this long to just build two new wings, then the full castle will take a lifetime. I shall settle with just this for now and am impatient that I will not be able to move my books into the tower before we leave again.

For we are leaving. It cannot wait any longer. Our journey to France was too short. I have waited and waited for her to recover, to come back into herself again and to no avail. I have waited and waited for them to finish the damn tower to no avail. I shall leave my steward to manage it. I am done. We are leaving for Russia. I need to go farther, somewhere uncharted by others from this country, somewhere I can write about and publish a book on. Somewhere far enough away that we cannot easily turn back.

Ann is still undecided as to whether to join me or stay behind. She talks of returning to her sister or at least to Crow Nest and having a succession of visitors there to keep her occupied, but she has done nothing to formally arrange either of these options, so it is just talk. In truth she does not want me to leave her; nor does she want to come with me. If only Marian were here to keep her company, then I could leave the two of them and have no pressures on how long I travel for or when I return. In my heart, do I really want to leave them here forever and never return? Or do I want to return when they have both found themselves husbands to whisk them away and out of my responsibility? How awful that my thoughts run to plans to be rid of them. I thought I could care forever, that our love would keep us strong, our bond of marriage, but the years sweep by and she is unchanged. We have not had intimate relations for nearly a year. She spends each night with me, but her body is no longer mine. We occasionally kiss but she stops me or cries or flies off about something I had done a week before that upset her and that I can do nothing about.

My lover has become my tormentor.

Miss Walker

Now Marian will decide our fate. We write to her and beg her to move back to Shibden, as it is her home too. We miss her. Anne loves her sister and we both want her here with us. We tell her that Anne wishes to go travelling and I am not well enough to go but she does not want to leave me alone. Anne believes Marian is more upset with her than with me, so may come if she believes it will only be me here.

Miss Lister

We tell her we will invite Ann's sister Elizabeth to stay here too, with the children. It should be nice to have some children in the Hall, wouldn't she like that? We tell Marian about the woodlands and the lake, which she must come and see in the warmth of summer. We beg her to claim her part of Shibden for herself. I enclose a sketch of the stone Lister lion and note on the back, 'Some semblance of Father perhaps? Our Lister lion'.

I ask Marian in another letter from me alone, would she wish Ann from our lives? If she would befriend Ann again, then she never has to see me. I will sacrifice Ann to her to make her happy, so neither of them must be alone. I beg her to agree that if she will not join us now, will she at least look after Ann should anything happen to me? Do not blame Ann for any of this, I tell her, it was all my doing.

We do not hear back for weeks.

I set a date to leave, with or without Ann, as the twentieth of June; to keep on waiting is insufferable. If I do not set off by summer, I shall have the worst of journeys through winter. The desire to leave burns inside me and I know she sees it, but I cannot help it. I seem to find no satisfaction in earthly pursuits and pleasures any more. Temporarily perhaps, but never to my core, as if everything stops at my skin. Travel presents itself as the only possible source for some enjoyment.

Miss Walker

She eventually writes back and agrees to visit! All is not lost, Marian will come. But she goes on to say that she will come for Christmas time. She believes as a family we should spend Christmas together, but she will come no sooner. There are no promises to move back in; it will just be a visit. Christmas is several months away, and Anne wants to leave in June. Marian will make us wait and she gives herself ample time to change her mind. Perhaps she says this just to stop our asking and intends to refuse us later. Anne fumes and shouts cruelly, what can she possibly have to fill the next seven months in her little life?

Some days I believe I can travel and look at the routes through Russia and beyond with Anne; I see myself there, with her, away from all the sadness here. But another day I will wake up with a fear in me that tells me I should not venture away from this place. If it were just to Europe again perhaps that would suit me, but she tells me she has finished with Europe and must go farther, especially for the travel book to be published; there are so many on European travels, she tells me, it must be somewhere new, that few have been to.

She makes it sound as if she must travel just to write about it. She talks of her readers as if they already exist. I suggest she should perhaps complete the article about her mountain ascent first and see how it is received, but this just riles her and she says it will not sell as Europe is not exotic, it's not far enough away. All I see is that she still has something to prove, to whom I'm not sure: herself, her sister, the Halifax set, her London friends, the world? Her solution is always to leave, to run away. But where can she ever truly run to and not find herself there?

Miss Lister

Without the world looking on we cannot be measured, examined, labelled, misunderstood or insulted. I see the appeal of building high walls and with this new venture overseas I will cut any remaining local ties. I shall finally forgo my pew at the church, and if we return I will build us our own chapel. I shall be satisfied with all I am fortunate enough to have and not seek again to meet new acquaintances. Shibden Hall itself will be our Moss House, our sanctuary, our private place.

Little Halifax is not ready for us. It cannot cope with anything but the ordinary and so will never grow to much. It shall remain a nondescript town on the route to nowhere with its layer of smog and forlorn buildings and sense of a prosperous past which it could not maintain, its simple-minded people going about their dull daily lives. There can be no real progress when half the population is still shackled to men, with no rights of our own, denied education and any chance to make the world anew. The new Queen has done nothing to change that, despite my high hopes.

Miss Walker

We've talked more of plans for when we return which comforts me, makes the trip sound more temporary, something I can endure knowing we will come home again once and for all. We talk of how we will remain at Shibden, possibly even sell Crow Nest and use the money to improve the Hall even more and for the first time in my life, never returning to Crow Nest does not fill me with dread or sorrow. After my years here at Shibden, it feels like home. When I visit Crow Nest these days it feels like a hotel.

After this trip we will live out our days contentedly, she assures me. We'll have her book published and we can put travelling behind us.

Hopefully Marian will come back to us and my sister will visit more often on our return – oh, how I miss her! I will be abandoning her for years with no one to even correspond with, for once we reach Russia, it could be weeks or months for post, and I will miss everything and be unable to help in any way. I can see why so few people travel; it is all-consuming, to be plucked from one's life and transported elsewhere with no definite return date, no idea what life will bring, both for us, the travellers, and those we leave behind. What if either of us falls ill, and the other is left to nurse them, to try to bring them home? I shall make myself ill with the worry of it. Both of us are now leaving our sisters to their fates, even though they are all we have left – a sister each whom we abandon for our own adventure. If only they could come too.

With no last-minute reprieve, no last-minute letter from Marian to rescue me by coming home to us, no letter from Elizabeth to say Sutherland has died and she is free to return, the day is upon us.

I check my bags and my trunk again. How is it possible to know what to take for two years? Everything, ideally, but nothing that can be too easily damaged or crumpled or suffer in adverse weather. Nothing too valuable in case it is stolen. Nothing too precious in case it is lost. I should just place myself in the trunk and have done. Lock myself inside it until we arrive.

I detest journeys. The confines of the carriage, the rocking of the ship, the packing and unpacking along the way, never being able to find what you need and the language around you that you do not understand. Eyes on you, judging you, no different from here at home, wondering who these two pale women are, arm in arm, and what we are doing in their country.

So fearful to leave but also to be left. I have become so reliant on Anne as if she is the very sun, and without her all I can see is darkness. To be left here without her is inconceivable. But so is Russia! A dark unimaginable place to which she forces me to accompany her.

I cannot stay here alone, but I cannot shake this feeling of foreboding that hangs over me about leaving.

Miss Lister

She enters the carriage as if being dragged to an asylum. I am not forcing her to come! I have given her fair chance to remain, offered to employ more staff, find a new companion for her, even convinced her aunt and Mrs Priestley to visit her more, take her under their wing. Yet she insists on coming with me.

I am accustomed to travel and so I shall be the husband, the tour guide, the guard of precious Ann once more. I squeeze her hand in reassurance and glance back at Shibden. The near-completed tower in which I cannot wait to place my books and write up the travels on which I am about to embark.

I am excited by the journey before me, but sad to leave Shibden behind. I will see you again soon, Shibden. I open the compass from Father, which I carry at all times; the needle turns and finds North. It will help me find my way home again, he said, but what is home when it is empty?

Now I had best reassure Ann, so we can at least be out of our own grounds before she starts to cry.

Miss Walker

I look once more at Shibden Hall through the carriage window as we set off down the driveway. Our home, our safe place, our Moss House, and suddenly the thought comes to me that only one of us will ever return here again.

Anne takes hold of my hand and, before we have even passed the gatehouse and joined the main road, I cannot help but cry.

Miss Lister

Dear God, what have I let myself in for?

Miss Walker

Dear God, please do not ever let her leave me.

Epilogue

Anne Lister and Ann Walker set off from Shibden Hall on the twentieth of June 1839 for their trip to Russia. They went to Belgium, Germany, Denmark, Sweden, Norway, Finland, Russia and Georgia, where Anne Lister died on the twenty-second of September 1840. Ann Walker was left alone to return with her partner's body, which was interred at Halifax Parish Church on the twenty-ninth of April 1841, seven months after Anne's death.

Ann Walker returned to Shibden Hall, which she had inherited from Anne, but on the ninth of September 1843 her brother-in-law Sutherland had Doctor Belcome forcibly remove her from Shibden and take her to an asylum in York. Sutherland moved into Shibden himself, seemingly alone. Elizabeth died in 1844.

On the twenty-fifth of February 1854, Ann died aged fifty at one of the Walker properties, Cliffe Hill. She left Marian an annual sum in her will and the rest of the Walker estate to Elizabeth's son, George. After Sutherland's death and a range of tenants while Ann was alive, Shibden's ownership returned to distant Lister family members in 1855. Marian Lister never returned to Shibden and died unmarried on the sixth of August 1882. Shibden was occupied until the last Lister resident died childless in 1933, and it was donated to the town of Halifax as a museum and public park. Mariana Lawton died without an heir in 1868.

By the time of her death, Anne had written over five million words in her diaries, along with fourteen volumes of travel notes and countless letters. Anne's diaries were first read by John Lister, the last Lister to live at Shibden, who published many edited extracts in the local newspaper. He also cracked Anne's secret code but never revealed any of its content. Anne's diaries, including the coded sections, were read again over the years by several different people. However, Anne's lesbian relationships remained secret until Helena Whitbread published sections from Anne's earlier diaries in 1988. Few people have ever read the diaries in full and no transcripts have yet been published or digitised. Very little is known about Ann Walker.

This fictional account is based loosely on known key dates and events. You can find out more about the real Anne Lister on Shibden Hall's website and in the introductory book *Anne Lister of Shibden Hall*, published by Calderdale Museums who look after the Hall.